*Sable Hamilton*

# STARDUST STABLES

## A Star Is Born

**STONE ARCH BOOKS**

a capstone imprint

Stardust Stables is published by Stone Arch Books
A Capstone Imprint
1710 Roe Crest Drive
North Mankato, Minnesota 56003
www.capstonepub.com

First published by
Stripes Publishing Ltd
1 The Coda Centre, 189 Munster Road
London SW6 6AW
Text © Jenny Oldfield, 2013
Cover © Stripes Publishing Ltd, 2013
Original horse and rider image © Living Images by Carol Walker, 2013
Stock photography © Shutterstock, 2013

Library of Congress Cataloging-in-Publication Data is available
on the Library of Congress website.

ISBN: 978-1-4342-9790-7 (library binding)
ISBN: 978-1-4342-9794-5 (paperback)
ISBN: 978-1-4965-0206-3 (eBook PDF)

Summary: New girl Kami is excited to start her first stunt riding job,
but she soon discovers that life at Stardust Stables isn't all glitz and
glamour.

Designer: Alison Thiele

Artistic Elements: Shutterstock

Printed in China.
092014      008472RRDS15

For Shelley, my fearless friend

# Chapter 1

"Hey, Kami. Welcome!" said Jack Jones, the co-owner of Stardust Stables, as he stretched a hand out.

Kami Cooper grinned at him. "Hey," she said.

She and her dad had just made the two-hour drive from their home in Elk Creek. They'd dropped off her bags in the girls' dorm, and then she'd waved goodbye to her dad. Day one at the Colorado stables had now kicked into action, and Kami was excited.

"Good timing," Jack told her. He was tall and lean, around forty years old, and his face was creased into a broad, welcoming smile. "Lizzie's working some of our horses and riders in the pen. Come take a look."

She followed him across the corral, past a squat red barn and a row of wooden stalls toward a fenced-in arena.

"Hey, guys," Kami whispered to the ponies

7

looking out over the stall doors — a pretty palomino, a high-class, bored-looking sorrel, a cute brown-and-white Paint, and a beautiful light gray Quarter Horse with a long black mane.

As the ponies nickered at the newcomer, a boy working in one of the empty stalls popped his head up over the wall. He was about fourteen years old, tall, slim, and was wearing a pale blue T-shirt and a baseball cap with the bill reversed to protect the back of his neck from the fierce sun.

"Hey, Tom," Jack said. "Meet Kami Cooper. Her folks run Elk Creek Guest Ranch a couple of hours southwest of here. She's joined us for the summer, so you'll be seeing plenty of her."

Tom nodded and gave Kami a quick smile.

"Tom's a regular member of our team," Jack explained. "This is his second season here, along with his sister, Kellie. They live thirty minutes away, just outside of Colorado Springs, so they get to work here during school vacations and on weekends, too."

"So, how did Jack and Lizzie find you?" Tom asked. He came out of the stall, brushing straw from his jeans, and followed Jack and Kami to the pen.

"I entered a contest in Clearwater County," Kami replied, looking away shyly. Tom's direct gaze and lazy drawl made her feel even more self-conscious than when she first shook hands with Jack. She blushed and swept her light blond hair forward to hide her face.

"Lizzie was in the area scouting for talent," Jack explained. "The Clearwater show attracts some terrific junior riders. Lizzie saw Kami win the barrel-racing contest by a mile and thought she'd be a great addition to our team."

"Awesome! Which horse will she be riding?" Tom asked.

Jack shrugged. "I have no idea — that's Lizzie's decision."

"Just as long as it's not Legend," Tom joked. "I'll fight anyone who tries to take my palomino away from me!" As they reached the arena fence, his gray eyes twinkling, he asked Kami, "So, you think you can make it as a stunt rider?"

"I don't know about that," Kami answered tentatively. This was all so new — the sunny corral nestled at the foot of the mountains, the big old barn to one side and the ranch house to the other, the round training pen on the near side of a fast-running creek. Beyond the creek there was a green meadow where horses grazed. And now there was this gangly boy with a mischievous smile and cute sticky-out ears asking questions and grinning at her.

"Sure you can — you're the best young rider

in your county," Jack said to her. "Your dad told Lizzie they put you in the saddle at the age of two."

"But I don't know any stunts," Kami said. She gasped as three riders galloped their mounts around the pen under Lizzie's instruction. "Not yet anyway," she finished.

The horses came so close she could almost reach over the fence to touch them. She caught the smell of sweat and dust and felt dirt that had been kicked up by the horses' hooves sting her cheeks.

"Hey!" A girl in a pink shirt on a sorrel mare waved as she galloped by, seemingly glued to the saddle. Her glossy, long, dark hair hung loose beneath her helmet, and she wore sunglasses to protect her eyes. Horse and rider in perfect harmony — it was beautiful.

"That's Alisa on Diabolo," Jack told Kami. "She's a pro. Watch and learn!"

"Hi, there!" A second girl greeted Kami from atop a dark bay Quarter Horse. She wore a yellow plaid shirt beneath a blue vest, and she rode her pony bareback.

"Kellie and Dylan," Tom said, taking over the introductions. "Kellie's my little sister. She's thirteen."

"The same age as me," Kami said. She watched with awe as Kellie suddenly switched from sitting to crouching on Dylan's hindquarters. Then she went from crouching to standing, her arms spread wide.

"Lizzie's teaching them a new trick," said Tom.

Kellie and Dylan caught up with Alisa and Diabolo, then Kellie leaned sideways and shifted her weight across so that she stood astride the two ponies.

"Roman riding," Jack explained, watching Kami's amazed reaction. "Kellie's a natural stunt rider. Now take a look at Hayley on Cool Kid."

Kami switched her attention to the third horse and rider — a stocky little Paint ridden by a skinny girl with a long, dark braid that made her look younger than the others. Her pony kicked up a cloud of dirt as she pulled him to a stop. She sprang from the saddle and gave Cool Kid a tap on his hindquarters. The pony set off again at a trot. Hayley chased after him, came alongside, then vaulted back into the saddle.

"Think you can do that?" Tom asked with a grin.

Kami frowned and shook her head. These girls were seriously good. Now Lizzie called in other riders — a couple more girls and some boys, until there was a total of ten riders working their horses in the pen.

"You will, no problem," Jack told her kindly.

"Everyone feels a little nervous at first. But you just have to put in the hours. Stunt riding is one part talent and three parts hard work."

Kami nodded as she watched riders fling themselves sideways, then hang from their saddles by their legs (which Tom told her was called a "drag") and riders clinging to the saddle horn and throwing their weight forward toward their pony's head (a "front wing"). They were exciting, dangerous stunts. Kami was afraid she'd never learn them.

"Lizzie, do you have time to introduce Kami to her pony?" Jack called out as his wife walked by.

"Hey, Kami!" Lizzie had been focused on teaching and hadn't noticed her arrival. She came out of the pen to greet her. "How was your trip? Did you drop off your stuff in the girls' dorm? You're rooming with Alisa — I'm sure she'll show you around. How about getting something to eat?"

"No, I'm good, thanks," Kami said. She was glad to say hi to a familiar face at last. She recognized Lizzie from Clearwater — she was short and slim, her hair tied back under a black Stetson and gold hoop earrings that added a touch of glamour to her western outfit that consisted of a dark plaid shirt, blue jeans, and tall, stylish riding boots.

"So, are you ready to meet the horse you'll

be working with?" Lizzie asked, picking up on Kami's excitement.

"Yes, please," Kami replied.

Lizzie gestured for Kami to follow and led the way across the corral toward the barn. "Don't be nervous," she said, turning to Kami with a smile. "His name's Magic. You're going to love him."

∽ ◦ ⌒

"I'm never going to be that good!" Kami told Magic. Lizzie had just gone to the office to order more grain for the horses, leaving Kami alone with her new horse in his straw-lined stall.

Magic nudged her gently with his nose. He was the horse who had caught her eye in the stalls earlier that morning — the pale, dappled gray one with the long, dark mane.

Now that she was close up, Kami saw that he had the biggest, gentlest brown eyes, the softest muzzle, and the longest, thickest, glossiest mane. Lizzie had been right — it was love at first sight.

"You know, it was tough leaving my pony, Buttercup, behind," she told him sadly. "She's back home in Elk Creek. I love her, too, of course. She's a gorgeous sorrel, and I've known her since I was eight. But there was no way I could bring Buttercup to Stardust. She's a working ranch horse, and my parents need her there to help. I won't see her again until I go back there in the fall. I'm going to miss her so much."

Magic gave her another nudge.

"I'm a decent rider," Kami confessed to him in a soft voice, trying to be positive. "But there's no way I'm as good as Alisa, Kellie, or Hayley. I'm no superstar."

The beautiful gray Quarter Horse rustled his feet in the straw.

Kami put her arms around his neck in the quiet warmth of his stall and sighed. "I just hope you're not going to be disappointed in me," she whispered.

Magic turned his head and nuzzled her cheek. His soft nose tickled, and she smiled.

"Yeah, I hear you," she murmured. "You're telling me not to worry — you and me, we're going to be a perfect fit!"

∽ ◦ ⌒

"So, Kami, how do you like your horse?" Alisa asked.

It was just after lunch. Alisa, Hayley, and Kellie had split off from the boys and invited Kami to join them at the soda machine behind the tack room. They took glasses of Coke and ice from the machine and then sat together around a rough wooden table, under the shade of a big yellow sun umbrella.

"I love him," Kami said, sighing. The drink was so cool. She needed it after two hours scooping up horse manure in the hot corral with Tom and two other boys named Zak and Ross.

"I can't believe my brother had you scooping poop," Kellie remarked. Her helmet had left a red mark around her forehead. Like Tom, she had clear gray eyes. "That's the worst job in the world!"

"Nope, the worst job would be walking out to the meadow at five in the morning to bring in the horses," Alisa disagreed. "I'm talking December — it's still dark, and the temperature's ten degrees below zero."

"But she still looks like she just stepped out of a Wrangler ad — not a hair out of place," Hayley joked.

"I do not," Alisa protested, but Kami believed Hayley. She'd already decided that her new roommate was just about the most elegant girl she'd ever met.

"Kami, I bet you thought stunt riding was all glitz and glamour," Hayley said. She laughed. "They didn't tell you about the poop."

"It's okay, I live on a guest ranch," Kami explained. "I'm used to it."

The three girls seemed super friendly, and Kami started to relax.

"We know," Kellie said. She had a round face and a big smile. "We also know you picked up first prize in barrel racing at the Clearwater show. You've been competing forever, since you were only five. We heard your whole story from my brother, Tom."

"Lizzie is a great scout," Alisa said. "She knows talent when she sees it. Jack's the one who has the contacts in movies and TV. Once upon a time he was an actor and stunt rider himself, so he knows directors and other actors in the business, plus the agents who find most of our work and sort out the contracts. He deals with the financial side of things."

"Lizzie and Jack work together on choreographing the stunts," Kellie explained. "They're both top names in the industry."

"Enough. I bet Kami already knows the history of Stardust!" Hayley cried, getting up from the table.

"No, I want to hear this," Kami said, taking another swig from her cup and settling down to listen to her new friends. This was going to be a great experience, she decided — learning amazing stunts and hanging out with the girls.

"Lizzie Jones is only the best horse trainer

this side of the Rockies, and she's into natural horsemanship methods, which means listening to what the horse is telling you and never using any force," Kellie explained.

"Which makes us totally respect her," Alisa added. "She married Jack three years back, just before he joined Stardust Stables. Now they're in competition with Lizzie's ex — a guy named Pete Mason. He's set up a rival stunt-riding stable named High Noon."

"Yawn, yawn," Hayley interrupted. "Come on, guys — there are horses to ride."

"No, Kami should know the basic insider facts," Alisa said.

Hayley shrugged her shoulders, then went to the corral to saddle up.

"It hasn't been easy for them to keep the business going," Alisa explained. "Especially since Pete often plays dirty by bad-mouthing Stardust and deliberately undercutting the fees we charge. In my book, that amounts to stealing work that should really come to us."

"So what Alisa is trying to say is that we never know for sure when the next big deal is coming," Kellie explained. "But, hey, until it does, we just train and train until our butts are sore!"

"Speaking of which," Alisa said as she got up from the table, "I have to slap a saddle on Diabolo and take him down to the creek. This afternoon Jack wants to rehearse the 'fall from the horse and land in water' trick."

"After that, he's teaching Dylan to ride through fire," Kellie added. "You might think I'm kidding, Kami, but I'm not!"

∽ ◦ ✑

"Never!" Kami promised Magic as she led him into the corral, tethered him to the fence, and started to saddle him up for her first session. "Never and no way will I ever take you near flames!" Horses hated fire — it was their worst nightmare.

"She talks to her horse!"

Kami swung around, blushing furiously. Tom was right behind her, leading his horse, Legend, into the corral.

"She talks to her horse and expects him to answer," Tom teased. "Actually, it's kind of cute."

Kami felt hotter and more embarrassed than ever. "Anyway, I *won't* take Magic near fire!" she declared. "I'd never do anything that would put my horse in danger."

Tom only looked at her and grinned. Then he turned to his horse. "You hear that, Legend? No fire stunts for Kami and Magic."

Legend, the palomino, tossed her blond mane.

"Legend says not to worry — there's always a rep from the American Humane Association on set," Tom said. "As the credits say: 'No animals were harmed in the making of this film.'"

There was something about Tom that made Kami smile. "I'm late. I have to meet Lizzie in the pen," she said. She untied Magic's lead rope and walked him out of the corral, feeling her stomach begin to knot up. What if it turned out she was no good at stunt riding? How could she bear to go home and admit to her mom and dad that she wasn't going to perform any daredevil tricks in front of the camera after all?

"Hey, Kami." Lizzie Jones was already there, smiling down from her beautiful sorrel mare. "This is Sugar. And don't worry — we won't try anything too tricky this afternoon."

Kami swallowed hard. She felt Magic walking calmly at her side. Knowing he was there gave her confidence as she fastened her helmet, then swung herself into the saddle. "Good boy," she whispered, and she squeezed her legs against his sides.

First task — trot around the arena so Lizzie could watch the movement of every muscle in horse and rider.

Second — squeezing her legs against his sides,

sitting low in her saddle, and clicking her tongue, Kami eased Magic into a trot around the rim of the pen.

By then, Tom had finished grooming Legend in the corral, and he and Zak had come to the fence to watch.

"Don't you have work to do?" Lizzie called when she spotted them.

"Nope," Tom insisted. "We're done."

"Well, just try not to draw attention to yourselves, however hard that might be," Lizzie said. She grinned and then gave Kami her next instruction. "Run Magic until he's totally relaxed."

Kami loved the smoothness of Magic's stride. She also loved his intelligence and basically everything about him. The sun shined down, sending the temperature soaring. Kami couldn't help smiling. This was as close to heaven as she ever hoped to get.

"Okay, the first stunt you're going to learn this afternoon is how to stand up in the saddle," Lizzie explained as she and Sugar came alongside. "Watch — I'll show you."

Kami concentrated hard as Lizzie kicked her feet free of the stirrups and pulled her knees toward her chest, then let go of the reins. As Sugar cantered on, Lizzie leaned forward and tucked her feet right under her. Then she raised herself into a standing position and kept her balance by spreading her arms wide. "See?"

Kami nodded. Her mouth was dry, her palms sweaty.

"Try the first part," Lizzie told her. "Kick your feet out of your stirrups, and let go of the reins."

Kami did it. Magic didn't miss a beat. His ears were swiveled back in her direction, waiting for her next move.

"Now bring your knees toward your chest," Lizzie instructed.

She did as Lizzie said. She was perched on the shiny saddle, but her balance wasn't quite right. Magic cantered on. Kami leaned into the bend.

"Lean out," Lizzie called. But it was too late.

Leaning into the curve, Kami lost control. Then, as she felt herself slipping, she tried to grab the saddle horn.

"Whoa!" Tom and Zak called as she hit the ground.

Kami lay there as Lizzie caught hold of Magic's reins and brought him to a halt.

"You okay?" Lizzie asked.

Kami nodded. The only thing that hurt was her pride. She stood up and dusted herself off, then took a deep breath. "Sorry," she mumbled. Forget the glamour of stunt riding — she realized this was going to be pure grind and sweat, plus cuts, bruises, and maybe even a cracked rib or two along the way.

"No problem," Lizzie said. "Are you ready to try again?"

"This time without eating dirt," Kami promised Magic, wiping the dust off her pants.

"You're not the first, and you won't be the last to fall off your horse when you're training to be a stunt rider," Lizzie said, grinning. "Come on, let's go again."

# Chapter 2

Night was the loneliest time.

Kami had been fine all day as she made new friends and bonded with Magic. But now that she was lying in bed and staring up at the sky as moonlight poured through the gap in the drapes, she missed her home so much it made her heart ache.

She missed her mom and her dad. She missed her cat, Squeaky, purring and licking her face to wake her up in the morning, and most of all, she missed her own sorrel pony, her beloved Buttercup.

The clock at her bedside ticked as she watched the clouds drift across the moon. All was quiet in the girls' dorms. Kami stared at the stars until at last her eyes closed, and she drifted off to sleep.

The stars were shining, and she was riding Buttercup through the spring meadow at Elk Creek, feeling the wind in her hair, hearing the thudding sounds of hooves on soft turf. Next thing she knew, the sun was up, and they were trotting through the creek, kicking up spray. Then they were way up in the mountains with no one else around, just relaxing and taking in the view of Clearwater Lake far below. She saw Buttercup's face close-up — her wonderful, dark eyes so gentle and trusting, the white flash running down her nose, the unruly, nut-brown mane that refused to fall neatly to one side.

"However hard I brush, I just can't get that to look right," Kami said with a sigh as she stepped up into the saddle and rode Buttercup proudly into the arena at the county show.

The crowd cheered, and Kami woke up with a start.

In the small, simple bedroom at Stardust, she heard the sound of Alisa's quiet, even breathing. There was nothing here but two beds, each with a nightstand and a lamp, and across the room, a shared closet. On the table next to Kami was a framed picture of her and Buttercup, proud winners of the county barrel-racing contest. Lying in the dark, Kami felt tears come to her eyes.

∾ ◦ ᵔ

"The first forty-eight hours are the worst,"

Kellie assured Kami over a breakfast of eggs, crispy bacon, and hash browns.

All the kids at Stardust Stables — twelve in total — were up at dawn and assigned to various chores before breakfast. Some brought horses in from the meadow, some got extra grain for the horses, some shifted bales of hay, and others scooped manure in the corral. Then they all ate breakfast with Jack and Lizzie in the old ranch house before starting their training routines.

At the start of Kami's second day, Kellie made a beeline for Kami as soon as she arrived in the dining room. "You look like you need to talk," she said.

"It's okay. I'm good," Kami insisted, even though her eyes stung from lack of sleep. She pushed the food around her plate without eating anything.

"No, you're not. You're homesick," Kellie said. She looked at Kami's plate. "Do you want those hash browns?" she asked her. When Kami shook her head, Kellie scooped the heap of fried potatoes onto her own plate.

"Anyway," Kellie went on, "we're all nervous the first time we come here. This is my third year at Stardust, but I remember my first time like it was yesterday."

"Hey, Kellie! Hey, Kami!" Alisa and Hayley

called across the noisy room. They were sitting with a girl Kami hadn't met yet. The girl was small and had blond hair like Kami's. She stared curiously at Kami from where she sat on the other side of the dining area.

"That's Becca," Kellie told Kami. "She's a great rider . . ."

"But?" Kami asked. She felt there was a "but" in there somewhere.

"No buts. Just know that Becca has been working with Lizzie forever. This is her sixth year. She's been in all the *River Eden* movies, plus the *Gold Rush* TV series. I could go on and on. So anyway, like I was saying — get through today, and you'll start to love it here, okay?"

"Thanks," Kami said. She gave Kellie a grateful smile. "Hey, I didn't get the chance to ask you yesterday — how did you and Dylan do riding through fire?"

Kellie shrugged. "Dylan was spooked by the flames, so we took it nice and slow. It turns out Jack thinks he may not be the best choice for scenes taking place in burning barns or whatever. Diabolo's better. Dylan's good with explosions, though, and no horse plays dead better than him."

"I've got so much to learn," Kami said. She thought through all the stunts she couldn't yet perform and sighed.

Kellie grinned and said, "So, what are you waiting for?" She shoveled down the last of the hash browns and marched Kami out of the dining room.

"Oh, and by the way, Tom really likes you," Kellie added, arching her eyebrows and grinning broadly. "He's a typical boy, so you'll never get him to admit it, but I'm his sister, and I know these things!"

∽ ◦ ᴄᴑ

Still blushing, Kami walked Magic in from the meadow and tethered him to a railing in the corral, where she picked up a brush and began working the caked dirt out of his dappled coat. Becca's horse, Pepper, stood beside them. He was also gray, similar to Magic but bigger and with a white mane and tail.

"Let me see that brush," Becca said, coming out of the tack room.

Kami handed it over and waited.

"This belongs to me and Pepper," Becca informed her without any trace of a smile. "Everyone has their own grooming kit. Yours is in the tack room on the shelf labeled 'Magic.'"

*Ugh*, Kami thought. She felt like she was two inches tall. She went inside and found Tom, Zak, and Ross sweeping out the tack room. The boys stopped talking the moment she arrived.

"Hey," Kami mumbled.

"Hey, Kami," Ross answered, while Zak elbowed Tom in the ribs and sent him sprawling behind the railing of halters.

Awkward! Remembering what Kellie had told her, Kami made a quick grab for Magic's brush and currycomb and headed back out to the corral.

Luckily, Becca had already saddled Pepper and was heading toward the pen, leaving Kami free to groom her pony until his dappled coat shone in the sunlight and his mane and tail were smooth and tangle-free.

*Relax!* She told herself. *This is only your second day. You can't expect to know how things work around here already.*

Magic tossed his head. Then he softly nuzzled her hand, as if to say, *"Stick with me, kid. We'll be totally fine!"*

Kami smiled and stroked his neck. She had his saddle on and was busy with his bridle when Tom stepped out onto the tack-room porch.

"Sorry, I don't want you to think we were talking about you back there," he mumbled shyly. Then his mischievous grin broke through. "Actually, we were, though. Zak and Ross were giving me a hard time."

"No problem," Kami said, grinning back at him. "I heard something similar from your sister."

"Jeez!" Tom said.

"Yeah," Kami replied.

"Anyway, I thought I'd just say hi," Tom said as he began to turn away.

"Yeah, hi!" Blushing furiously, Kami stepped into the saddle and followed Becca and Pepper into the pen.

"Good luck," Tom called after her. "You're going to do great — trust me!"

∽ ◦ ⌒

"At Stardust, we work as a team," Lizzie reminded Kami and Becca. Lizzie was on foot, ready to teach Kami how to stand in the saddle. "Becca, you're going to ride Pepper alongside Magic, showing Kami exactly what to do. Kami, you're going to copy Becca move for move."

The girls nodded.

"Don't overthink this," Lizzie advised Kami. "Relax and be confident that you can do whatever I ask. And remember — keep your eyes on Becca. She, along with Alisa, is the most experienced junior stunt rider we have."

Another nod from Kami, and they were ready to go, side-by-side, from walk into trot and then into canter. The horses moved perfectly in time as Lizzie stood in the center of the pen and called out instructions. "Kick out of the stirrups! Drop your reins!"

The horses cantered on while both girls did as Lizzie said. "Pull your knees toward your chest!" the instructor called.

Kami copied Becca, this time making sure that she didn't shift her weight.

"Now stand!" Lizzie called.

Kami glanced sideways to see Becca make one smooth movement from sitting to standing. She held her breath and copied.

Wow! This time she was actually keeping her balance and standing on the saddle. Magic was trotting on.

"Good!" Lizzie called. "Okay, now sit."

Kami had to look hard to see what Becca did. It involved keeping your back straight and bending your knees, then sliding back down into the saddle — smoothly.

Ouch!

"Not so good!" Lizzie groaned as Kami thudded down into the saddle. "But you get the general idea."

Glancing sideways, Kami thought she saw a smug grin flit across Becca's face. Then again, she could have imagined it.

"Do it again," Lizzie urged. "And this time, Kami, let's make that transition from standing to sitting a little smoother . . . for the sake of your poor butt, if nothing else!"

∽ ◦ ↺

"We really need to secure that *Moonlight Dream* contract before Pete steps in and grabs it from under our noses," came Lizzie's voice from a nearby table.

Kami was three days into her training when she overheard a conversation between Jack and Lizzie at breakfast on Thursday morning. It was her first morning off, and she'd slept in. The dining room was almost empty. She glanced around, wondering where Alisa and the rest had gone.

"I've been looking at our spreadsheets," Lizzie said to Jack. "Our profits are way down compared to this time last year."

Jack thought for a while, then said, "Matt Harrison is working on the *Moonlight* movie. I worked with him ten years back. You want me to call him?"

"Do you think he can help?" Lizzie asked.

Jack shrugged. "He could at least put Stardust's name in the hat instead of leaving everything in the hands of our agent, the way we usually do," he said.

"It's worth a try," Lizzie agreed. "But Matt's only an actor in the movie — it's not his decision."

"Sure, it's up to the director, Brad Morley," Jack replied. "And I know for a fact he's been having a hard time finding the right stunt double for the lead actress, Coreen Kessler."

"Okay, so call Matt," Lizzie said as she looked up to see Kami hovering uncertainly with her plate of eggs and wheat toast. "Come sit," she invited, making room for Kami at the table. "We won't talk business — I promise!"

Jack smiled. "I hear you're making good progress, Kami," he said.

"Yeah, tell Jack what you've learned in three short days," Lizzie urged.

Kami counted the stunts on her fingers. "Standing in the saddle — check. Roman riding — check. Front wing — check. And I have the cuts and bruises to prove it," she said, laughing.

"I'm impressed," Jack said. He grinned. "No regrets?"

Kami shook her head. "I still have a lot to learn, but I'm definitely having fun, and I'm making some great new friends."

"You like the horse we chose for you?" he asked.

"Magic is perfect," Kami said, smiling.

"How's the homesickness?" he inquired.

"Not too bad, thanks. I miss my horse back home, though," Kami replied. *And my cat, and my mom . . .*

"The good news is she'll still be there waiting for you in the fall," Jack said. He obviously understood and tried to make Kami feel better. "Until then, we'll do our best to keep you busy. Who knows, if you work hard enough, there could be a part for you in this major movie we were discussing."

"But no pressure," Lizzie broke in with a laugh. "Especially not today. Why not just relax? Some of the girls have already packed a bagged lunch and gone for a ride."

"Really?" Kami hadn't realized quite how long she'd stayed in bed.

"Alisa said to tell you where they were headed," added Jack. "Ride Magic along the creek, and you'll catch up soon. By the way, that horse should have been born a fish, the way he loves the water."

"Cool!" Kami said, grabbing her favorite straw Stetson she'd brought with her. She jumped up from the table. "Thanks."

Jack and Lizzie smiled. "This is your chance to do your own thing," Lizzie insisted. "You've worked hard — you deserve it."

∾ ◦ ∽

Jack was right — Magic was totally at home in the water.

He stepped into the clear, fast-running creek and was soon up to his belly. Kami had to pull her feet out of the stirrups to keep her boots from getting wet. She laughed as Magic waded on toward an island covered in thick willows.

"How cool is this!" Kami said to herself.

*Clunk!* Magic's hoof kicked a submerged rock. The rock dislodged, then hit another one.

"Whoa!" Kami shouted. She clung to the saddle horn as her horse lurched sideways, then righted himself.

Magic glanced around, as if to say, *"How about a swim?"*

Kami laughed. "Let's get to that island up ahead and see if we can find the girls," she told him.

Kicking him on, she looked ahead and saw that she and Magic were on the right track.

"Hey, sleepyhead!" Hayley called as she and Cool Kid emerged from the bushes. "Good sleep? Alisa said you were still snoring when she left." She held up a brown paper package. "Do you want to share my lunch?"

"Sure," Kami said. She was glad to catch up with them, as was Magic, who nickered a friendly greeting to the brown-and-white Paint.

Up ahead, Alisa led Diabolo out of the willows and waved at Kami.

"Kellie couldn't make it," Alisa explained as Magic reached the island and Kami dismounted. "She and Dylan are auditioning for a TV director. They want him to play dead for an old-style shoot-out scene between a girl on horseback and a no-good cattle rustler."

"All in a day's work at Stardust Stables," Hayley said, grinning. She opened up her lunch and offered Kami a bag of chips and a cheese sandwich. "And here's an apple for your horse," she added, handing it to Kami.

Magic spotted the treat, and his nostrils twitched. He craned his neck toward Kami's palm, grabbing the apple between his teeth and crunching loudly.

"Pretty perfect, huh?" Hayley said as Kami sat down on the grass and gazed down the creek. "Especially without the boys hassling us."

Kami nodded. Being out with the girls made her feel totally relaxed.

Water gurgled over the smooth stones and parted and gushed around the sides of pink granite boulders that rose from the water. Wildflowers grew along the banks — yellow spears of Indian tobacco plants, red poppies, and blue columbines. Above their heads, a strong sun hung in a pure blue sky, promising another scorching day ahead.

Kami smiled. This was the life! She was sitting with great new friends in a beautiful setting. Sure, the riding was challenging and the tricks were dangerous, but she had the best little stunt horse in the world by her side.

"So you're over being homesick, and you're going to stay the whole six weeks?" Alisa asked.

Kami swallowed and nodded. "I'm going to learn every stunt in the book," she promised. "And if Jack and Lizzie ask me, Magic and I are going to audition for *Moonlight Dream*."

"You're a good fit," Alisa assured her. "You could be Coreen Kessler's twin."

"More than Becca," Hayley added. "But don't tell her I said that!"

"Becca will definitely want that gig," Alisa commented. "But she's a little bit too tall to double for Coreen."

Kami nodded. "I'll keep my fingers crossed," she said.

Hayley grinned. "Good! I bet that one job could solve the current Stardust cash-flow problem."

"Until the next crisis," Alisa pointed out with a sigh. "Seriously, Kami, you could totally do it.

You look exactly right, which none of the rest of us do, and you've sure got the guts and the talent. So forget about Becca maybe wanting the same gig. Just go out there and win it — we'll be right behind you."

"Okay, if it happens, I'll do it," Kami vowed as they finished their lunches and climbed back into their saddles. She and Magic led the way into the creek. "Hey, I'm glad I caught up with you guys," she said. "This was fun."

"Likewise," Hayley said. She brought Cool Kid alongside, and Alisa and Diabolo followed close behind.

"How about a canter?" Alisa suggested as they reached a stretch of smooth sand.

Kami squeezed Magic's sides and felt him surge ahead, kicking up spray as he went. Cold water splashed her, and soon she was soaked from head to foot.

"Go, girl!" Hayley called from behind.

So Kami let Magic continue on through the creek, between the banks lined with wildflowers.

# Chapter 3

That afternoon it was back to serious work.

Jack had gathered the young riders at Stardust to practice vaulting on and off their horses.

"Hayley, go ahead and show the others how it's done," he instructed from where he was perched on the high fence. He wore a black cowboy shirt with white piping and, like Lizzie, a black Stetson to keep the sun off of his lean face.

Kami and the others gathered in the center while Hayley swung out of the saddle and sent Cool Kid loping around the rim. The sturdy pony snorted and kicked up dirt while Hayley stood in one spot, watching him closely. After his second circuit, she made her move. She sprinted toward him, landing both hands flat on his broad rump, then vaulted from behind, right into the saddle.

*Wow!* Kami resisted the urge to cheer and clap. She watched as Hayley cantered Cool Kid in one complete circuit before she hitched herself out of the saddle and smoothly vaulted off the back of her horse. *She's as limber as an Olympic gymnast,* Kami thought, *and she made a really difficult trick look easy.*

"So, Kami, do you think you know how to do that now?" Jack asked. When she nodded, he told her to go ahead and demonstrate.

Kami took a deep breath, trying her hardest to ignore Tom and Ross's raucous calls of "Yeah! Go, Kami!"

It was way harder to focus when people were watching you, but she knew it was something she would have to learn to deal with. She stood still and sent Magic off on a canter around the arena, watching the rhythm of his slow, easy stride until he passed where she stood — once and then a second time. Then she counted to three and set off after him, tucking in behind him, getting ready to spring up and place both hands on his hindquarters to leapfrog onto his back. But it was tricky, and she mistimed it, missing her chance as Magic cantered past.

"Stand back, wait for him to come around one more time," Jack called.

*Okay, next time I'll nail it,* Kami told herself. She watched Magic come past her again, and she set off. She tucked in close behind, then sprang forward. This time she pulled off the tricky vault. Now all she had to do was canter Magic for one full lap, then vault down to the ground . . .

"Yeah!" Hayley called as Kami reversed the sequence and landed smoothly.

"Good job!" Tom cried.

*Not perfect*, Kami thought, but she smiled anyway, letting out a huge sigh of relief.

"Now Becca, your turn," Jack called. "Do it exactly the way you did it last summer for the *River Eden* movies."

As Becca eased Pepper past Kami and Magic, Kami smiled. "Good luck," she said.

"Luck has nothing to do with it," Becca retorted. "We're talking skill and experience. Remember?"

Kami blushed. Why, oh why, did Becca have to make her feel so small?

"Don't let her get to you," Kellie said, easing Dylan alongside Kami and Magic. "She's only doing it because she's jealous."

"Of me?" Kami was shocked.

"Yes, of you." Blunt as ever, Kellie spelled it out for Kami. "Think about it — you two could be sisters. You have the same blond hair and blue eyes. Sure, Becca's a little taller, and she's one year older, which counts for a lot in this junior section of the business. But she still sees you as her main rival."

"But that's crazy," Kami protested as she watched Becca perform a perfect vault into the saddle. "She's a great rider."

"With a ton of experience as a stunt double,"

Kellie agreed. "But that doesn't stop her from looking at you and being very afraid!" She made her voice sound spooky for the last two words, then she giggled. "Anyway, Kami, ask me if Dylan got the cattle-rustling job."

"Did he get the job?" Kami asked as Becca finished her session and Jack called for Tom and Legend.

"He did!" Kellie crowed. "We get to go on location to Texas as soon as they finalize the date!"

∽ ◦ ⌒

"My little sister gets to go to Texas while I stay here scooping poop!" Tom complained.

He, Zak, and Kami were shoveling poop into a pile for Jack to drive out to the manure heap at the far end of the meadow. Ross, Kellie, and Alisa were cleaning tack while Becca wrote down the names of horses who needed new shoes.

"How come we get the worst job? Again!" Tom said. He made a big deal of the smelly task, but only to get a smile from Kami, who worked happily beside the boys.

"Dude, no whining!" Zak warned. "Remember, me and Ziggy almost got sent to Montana for the *Drifter* movie . . . until Lizzie's ex got a kid from High Noon in there instead. But do I feel bitter?"

"Yep," Tom grunted, still grinning at Kami as he shoveled an extra-heavy load and then tipped it out onto the pile.

"Okay, so I wish I was in Montana. Who wouldn't?" Zak stopped raking to lift his hat and wipe his brow with the back of his hand. "From what I hear, Pete Mason went in with a lower deal, and these days, it's money that does the talking. But the kid who got the job can hardly do even the simplest stuff. I saw him once at my local rodeo. He was totally unimpressive."

"Are we done here?" Tom asked, loading the final shovelful onto the trailer. "'Cause if we are, there's a bale of alfalfa ready to go out to the meadow."

Wearily, Kami laid down her shovel and headed toward the barn with Zak and Tom. She glanced at her watch and saw that there was still an hour to go before supper.

"Not wimping out, are we?" Tom challenged with his ready grin.

"No!" Kami said. She took a swipe at him with her straw hat and ran ahead. "Race you!" she called.

They reached the barn door together, but Tom shoved her sideways against a stack of straw bales, meaning that he was first to reach the tractor loaded with alfalfa for the horses. He jumped up behind the wheel.

Covered in straw and breathless from her sprint across the yard, Kami let Zak climb up beside Tom. "You two go," she told them. "I'll stay here and give Magic some grain."

"You spoil that horse!" Tom called as he trundled the tractor out of the barn to deliver dinner to the horses waiting at the meadow fence.

"I sure do," Kami admitted. She went to the grain store and scooped the small pellets into a bucket. Then she walked toward the stall where Magic was waiting. "Supper!" she announced, tipping the grain into the manger.

Magic nickered, raising his head and curling back his top lip in what looked like a smile.

∽ ◦ ⌣

After she fed her horse, Kami headed for the tack room. She'd just fetched Magic's bridle when she overheard Lizzie in the middle of a phone call.

"Okay, Matt, thanks. Really — thanks for trying." There was a pause, then she spoke again. "I should've known my ex would undercut us. These days, the director and the head wrangler don't care so much about the quality of the riding. It's all down to money. And Pete's done this before. Yeah, I hear you . . . yeah, you'll remind Brad that we're just down the road. That'd be good. Bye."

Lizzie sighed as she hung up the phone. When she spotted Kami, she shook her head and said, "It looks like the *Moonlight Dream* contract has slipped through our fingers . . . bad luck."

Kami frowned, but what could she say?

"Hey, not your problem," Lizzie said more cheerfully. She took the bridle out of Kami's hands and pointed her toward the door. "Magic's tack is already super clean," she insisted. "Look — it's totally gleaming. So go inside and relax."

∽ ⊙ ℃

"Sideways or back vault?" Tom asked.

It was early next morning, and Kami had ridden Magic bareback into the pen to practice her vaults. It was only eight a.m., and she was surprised that Tom and Legend had beat her there.

"Back," she replied, deciding this was the trick she still wanted to perfect.

"You want me to comment?" he asked.

Kami nodded. "Just don't make fun of me."

"Me?" Tom swung down out of the saddle and tethered his palomino to the fence. Then he folded his arms across his chest, ready to judge Kami's vault. "Okay. Look at my face, I'm dead serious."

"Now you're making me nervous," Kami complained as she set Magic off at a steady canter.

"Better get used to an audience. Think of all the people on a movie set — actors, techies, director . . ." Tom trailed off.

"Enough already!" Kami said.

As Magic cantered twice around the pen, Kami forgot about Tom and focused on her back vault. She'd learned yesterday that in this trick, timing was everything. She waited for her horse to pass her a third time, then she set off at a run, catching up to him and raising both arms to place her palms flat on his rump. She vaulted onto his back smoothly.

Magic kept on, steady as a rock.

"Good boy!" Kami murmured, leaning forward to pat his dappled neck. Then she drew him to a halt next to Tom. "Well?" she asked breathlessly.

He looked up at her with a twinkle in his gray eyes. "Work hard and you'll be . . ." he said, trailing off. After a pause, he broke out in the biggest grin this side of the Rockies. " . . . the best stunt rider at Stardust!"

*The best!* Kami laughed, and then she and Magic continued on. As they passed the gate, she saw two strangers walking across the parking lot to watch. Remembering Tom's advice not to let an audience distract her, she and Magic carried on with a vaulting dismount. Kami followed that up with a second vault, but this time from a sideways angle. Then she rode up close to the visitors, the wind flapping at her plaid shirt and tugging at her hair.

"Who's this?" Kami heard one of the men ask Tom as he pointed in her direction.

"That's Magic and Kami. Kami's new," Tom explained.

"She sure looks right," the other guy commented to his companion.

Suddenly Kami realized these visitors might be important, and she slowed Magic to a trot.

"Hello, my name's Brad Morley," the first guy announced as they trotted by.

Kami recognized the name of the famous movie director and gulped. She reined Magic back, then vaulted smoothly off his back.

"I'm taking time away from the desk part of my job," the director explained. "Scott, our head wrangler on *Moonlight Dream*, is busy with another job, so I invited Matt and a couple of other actors from the movie to come scouting for talent with me. We were heading down the road to High Noon Stables, but Matt here told me we should come take a look at Stardust first," Brad continued. "Now I want you young riders to prove that we're not wasting our time."

∽ ◦ ∾

After that, it was all action. Lizzie and Jack hurried out of the ranch house to greet their guests. Tom ran off to round up as many Stardust horses and riders as he could find. Soon Alisa and Diabolo, Zak and Ziggy, and Becca and Pepper had joined Kami and Magic in the pen.

"I'm trying to convince Brad that the cheapest deal isn't always the best," Matt explained to Jack after the two had shaken hands. They watched as Lizzie made the rest of the introductions.

The director, who was small and bald, with heavy-rimmed glasses, nodded at each of the riders, but looked nervous around horses. "Actually, we're looking for two stunt doubles for *Moonlight Dream*," he explained to Lizzie. "A boy and a girl. I need to get it exactly right in terms of riding ability and physical similarity to our leading actors."

"We'd be happy to show you a few basic stunts," Lizzie told him eagerly. "Then you can judge for yourself if we can give you the right combination."

Turning to the gathered horses and riders, Lizzie gave them all an encouraging smile. "Don't be nervous," she told them. "Keep your focus and trust your horse. And most importantly, have fun!"

*Oh, jeez!* Kami put her arm around Magic's

neck. This was her first audition, and it had come much sooner than she'd expected. Beside her, Becca stood cool as a cucumber with the sun shining prettily on her long blond hair. Beyond them, Zak followed Lizzie's instruction to break away from the group and demonstrate a couple of stunts on Ziggy.

"Give us a spin-the-horn, then go straight into a front wing," she told him.

Zak nodded and eased Ziggy into a trot. The Appaloosa held steady as Zak placed his palms flat on the saddle horn, took his weight all the way forward onto his hands, then executed a complete turn, like a gymnast on a pommel horse. With hardly a second to regain his breath, he then clutched the horn with his right hand and flung himself out of the saddle toward Ziggy's head.

Over by the fence, Matt applauded, and Brad nodded his approval. "What about the kid who was riding the gray one in here when we first arrived?" the director asked. Kami felt a quick jolt of disappointment as the director glanced at the riders and picked Becca and Pepper out of the group. "There you are, honey. Let me take another look at you."

"It wasn't Bec—" Tom began, but a fiery glance from Becca stopped him.

Unaware of the error, Jack talked up their

experienced rider, who quickly set Pepper off from a standing start into full gallop. "Becca's a seasoned stunt rider," he said. "She worked on *River Eden* and *Gold Rush*."

Brad nodded and watched with interest.

"Okay, Becca, go for a one-foot drag!" Lizzie called.

Becca nailed the athletic stunt perfectly, flinging herself from the saddle and allowing herself to be dragged in the dirt for five strides before kicking her foot free from the stirrup. She jumped to her feet, then picked up her hat and dusted herself off.

Standing on the sidelines, Kami watched with a sinking heart as Brad clapped and Becca gathered up Pepper's reins before walking back toward the group. As she came to a stop, she looked Kami in the eye. It was a look that said, *Beat that, newbie!*

"It's going well so far," Matt confided in Jack as the director took out a camera and snapped some close-up shots of Becca and Pepper. "My guess is that Brad will want to audition a couple more riders here before we move on to High Noon."

"Is he visiting any other stables aside from these two?" Lizzie asked anxiously.

"No," Matt assured her. "We fly back to California the day after tomorrow to continue filming. This is kind of a working vacation for us.

Hey, if you glance over your shoulder to see who's getting out of the car, I'd say the excitement of our visit is about to kick up a notch."

All eyes swiveled toward the yard where director Brad Morley's black SUV was parked. Two figures stepped out, both wearing dark glasses, both incredibly glamorous. The boy was tall and skinny, dressed in a loose, white cotton shirt over dark denim jeans and bright red Converse shoes. The girl was blond and in Western dress — a white leather jacket, fringed and studded, plus Wranglers and fancy, Cuban-heeled cowboy boots.

"Would you look at that!" Alisa said, her gaze fixed on the handsome face behind the Ray-Bans.

"That," said Becca, "is Nathan Atwood." For once, even she seemed impressed.

"And Coreen Kessler!" Tom added. If he'd been a cartoon, a string of shiny red hearts would have pulsated out of his chest. "I'm in love!" he gasped.

"Hey, guys, hurry on over here!" Brad called.

Nathan and Coreen picked up speed to join the director, while Kami stood next to Magic, feeling as if she wanted to fade into the background.

"Are you glad you came along for the ride?" Matt asked them.

Nathan nodded. "Hey, y'all," he said, his southern drawl breaking the hushed silence. "Dude, I couldn't stay in the car a minute longer. I just love your horse," he told Tom, giving Legend a stroke down the length of his nose. Then he picked out Alisa and asked her how long she'd been stunt riding and whether she got any time off for socializing.

"Hey," Coreen said, looking at no one in particular. She didn't reach out to any of the horses. She just stood in her white jacket, fringes swaying, studs gleaming, dazzling everyone with her perfect smile.

"They may be big names in the movies and starring in a multi-million-dollar teen romance," Brad confided in Lizzie and Jack, "but neither of these kids have ever ridden a horse before."

Jack stepped in quickly. "You want us to give them a few basics?" he asked.

Brad nodded. "Why not, since they're here and they'll have to sit on a horse for a few location shots? Matt told me on the drive over that you guys are good teachers. And I trust his judgment on horsemanship," he said.

"Come and get fitted for saddles," Lizzie said to Coreen and Nathan. "Tom and Alisa, fetch Sugar and Liberty. We'll have you up in the saddle soon, looking like you were born to ride!"

# *Chapter 4*

"It sounds crazy," Lizzie told Nathan as he sat on Liberty for the very first time. "But the way to ride a horse well is to learn how to think like a horse."

Nathan looked confused. "Run that by me one more time?" he said.

Lizzie smiled up at him. "The key is to recognize his way of looking at the world," she explained. "A horse in his natural life belongs to a large herd. So he doesn't like being out there alone because the prairie, the mountains, the desert — they're all full of hidden dangers. If you're on his back and asking him to separate from his buddies, he has to be able to trust you big time."

"I hear you," Nathan said. He was relaxed in the saddle, and Kami and the other riders from Stardust Stables could see that he was a natural. He didn't grip the reins too tight or press the bit against the horse's tongue, and he didn't tense up when Lizzie let go of the reins, letting Liberty walk across the pen.

"Good job," Lizzie called.

"He looks cool in Tom's cowboy boots," Alisa whispered to Kami. "And Ross's Stetson fits him just right."

"Anyone would look cool on Liberty," Becca pointed out. The dark bay gelding's coat shone like velvet, and he held his head high and proud.

"Don't be picky," Alisa said. She sighed. "Leave me be, and let me worship the ground Nathan Atwood walks on!"

Meanwhile, Jack tried to persuade Coreen to ride Sugar. "She's really safe," he explained. "Once you understand the basic rules, you'll do just fine."

But Coreen frowned and shook her head. "I paid a fortune for this jacket and my boots," she said. "I don't want to get them messed up."

"You don't want to ride?" Jack asked.

"Not right now," Coreen confirmed, and then she wandered back to the car.

"Hey, Coreen, this horse feels fine!" Nathan called to her as she walked away. "You want to try him?"

She shook her head again.

"I rarely come across a horse who isn't fine, once the rider understands the basic rules," Lizzie said, tilting Nathan's heels down and his toes up, then adjusting the reins a little. She walked them on, keeping a steady hand on Liberty's halter. "Watch Liberty's ears. If they're flicked toward you like they are now, it means he's paying attention, waiting for you to give him the next instruction."

"How do I do that?" Nathan asked. Now that he was at ease in the saddle, he was ready for more.

"If you want him to keep walking straight ahead, squeeze with both legs — good," Lizzie coached. "Keep your heels down, hold your balance, don't let your shoulders go up — well done!"

"It's too bad Coreen doesn't want to give it a try," Tom said to Zak as he leaned against the fence in bare feet. "I'd give her horseback riding lessons any time she wants — for free!"

"Dream on!" Zak laughed.

While Lizzie worked with Nathan, Matt took Brad aside for a private conversation, but they were close enough to Kami for her to catch snippets of their conversation. "So, what do you think?" she heard Matt say.

"Great little rider . . . gray horse . . . but we'd have to hammer out a deal," she heard Brad say.

"Talk to Lizzie and Jack," Matt advised. "They're good people, and they know their horses . . . I've worked with Jack, way back."

The director looked at his watch. "We still have to look at Pete Mason's riders," he reminded Matt. "Tell Jack we'll come back tomorrow." Taking his phone from his pocket, he walked swiftly toward his car, head down and talking fast.

Meanwhile, inside the pen, Nathan was feeling confident enough to try his first canter.

"Sit firmly in the saddle," Lizzie advised. "You need to feel like your butt is glued to the leather."

"His butt!" Alisa echoed, sighing as she faked a fainting fit.

Kami propped Alisa upright as she saw Becca shoot Alisa a warning glance.

"What?" Alisa protested. "If you think I'm bad, what about Tom and Zak? They couldn't take their eyes off Coreen!"

"Honestly, you'd think they'd never met a movie star in their whole lives," Becca said scornfully. "We're always working with famous actors at Stardust — what's the big deal?" Then her gaze fell on Kami. "Oh, except you," she added. "I forgot you just got here."

Two inches tall again and groaning inwardly, Kami didn't argue. *Face it — Becca stole my spot*, she thought, leaning her head against Magic's neck. *I never got the chance to do a real audition, so if anyone gets this job, it's going to be her.*

Magic turned and gently nuzzled her hand.

"Oops!" Alisa's voice burst Kami's bubble of sadness.

Nathan had just misjudged a bend and taken his first involuntary dismount. As he lay in the dirt laughing, it seemed this movie star was only human — he fell off of his horse just like everyone else.

∽ ◦ ⌇

"Why so quiet?" Hayley was the first to join Kami at supper and ask her what was the matter. She sat down next to Kami, then gestured for Alisa and Kellie to join them.

"No reason. I'm good," Kami said, trying to sound cheerful. But who was she kidding? On the inside, she was still hurting from the injustice of seeing Becca being picked for the tryout, when she hadn't even been given a shot.

In fact, she was so upset, Kami hardly noticed Alisa and Kellie come over and sit down.

"So you're not eating your steak, you've barely said a word since Brad Morley drove off, and you still say there's no problem?" Hayley persisted.

"Yeah, Kami, spill," Kellie urged. Tonight her wavy brown hair was pulled up in a high ponytail, and she wore a denim jacket over her green and blue plaid shirt.

"Tom told me what happened this morning," Alisa said.

"Well? What did happen?" Kellie and Hayley demanded.

Alisa lowered her voice. "Becca took the credit for some vaults that Kami and Magic performed in front of Brad," she said. "Tell them, Kami."

But Kami shook her head. "He made a mistake. He thought Becca was me — end of story."

Alisa shook her head. "Kami didn't even get the chance to audition," she told the others.

"But Becca did?" Kellie got it at last.

Kami nodded. "And she's a great rider," she said. "What chance do I have now?"

"From what I heard through the grapevine, there's no decision until Brad comes back for a second look tomorrow morning," Kellie pointed out. "That means he must want to do more auditions."

Alisa raised a hand to bring an end to the speculation. "Kami, there are a few things you need to understand about being at Stardust Stables. Number one, we're all great riders. That's not arrogant. It's a fact. Number two — and this is important," she said. "All of us are competing for jobs with one another."

"Yeah. We're friends, but we're also rivals," Kellie agreed. "Just two weeks back, Alisa and

Hayley were up for the same role in a movie called *Wild Mustang*. They both went to audition out in California. Alisa got the job, Hayley didn't. Alisa did three days' filming in the desert while Hayley schlepped back here with Cool Kid. But you don't see them fighting over it, do you?"

Kami shook her head.

"That's the way it is," Kellie said.

"And we're not *afraid* to compete," Alisa concluded. "What I'm saying is, you and Becca are definitely both up for the Coreen Kessler stunt-double role, just as soon as you register on Brad Morley's radar. Anyone with half a brain can see that. You both look the same as Coreen, you are both amazing riders . . ."

"But —" Kami began.

"No buts!" Hayley broke in. "You only have to get one thing inside your head and it's this — if you're lucky enough to go up against Becca for this role, you don't think twice . . . you go, girl!"

∽ ◦ ⌒

They made it sound so easy, Alisa, Kellie, and Hayley. But for Kami it was more complicated. For a start, she couldn't get Becca's sneaky put-downs out of her mind. And second, she was feeling pretty homesick again.

"You seem a little down," her mom said when Kami called her right after dinner.

"I'm good," Kami told her.

"Sure?" her mom asked.

"Yeah, I'm fine," Kami replied.

"Well, we're all good here, too. Buttercup's doing well on the guest string. Your dad brought in three new horses from the stock show over in Clearwater. There's a little Paint that you're just going to love," her mom explained.

"Cool," Kami said.

"And guess what — Squeaky's pregnant!" she continued. "We think the kittens will arrive later this month. We won't name them until you get back, though."

"Wow, that's great. I'm sad I won't see them being born, though," Kami said.

"So, what's your news, honey? Did you learn any more stunts?" her mom asked.

"Yeah, and today I met my first famous movie star — two, actually. Coreen Kessler and Nathan Atwood came to the stables."

"Oh, Kami!" Her mom was really excited for her. "You must be over the moon," she said. "Is there any chance you'll get to work with them?"

∽ ◦ ⌒

"I wanted to say no," Kami admitted to Magic as she walked in the moonlight with him. She'd come right out to the meadow after the phone call to tell him how she felt. "I wanted to ask Mom to let me come home, forget all about stunt riding . . . let me ride Buttercup out on the trails and be there when Squeaky has her kittens."

Magic walked beside her, his hooves brushing through the lush green grass. The moon cast a silver light onto his pale gray coat.

"No offense to you," Kami told him, stopping to put an arm around his neck before they walked on together. "But instead I told Mom there was still a slim chance I'd get to work on *Moonlight Dream*, and she sounded so . . . proud!" Kami sighed. She had to bite her lip to stop it from trembling. "So, even though I'm homesick, I've decided to stay and cowboy up."

Magic walked on steadily, his tail swishing, dark eyes gleaming.

"With you," Kami added. "I told Mom how awesome you are, how we went through the creek together, and how I'm learning all these tricks. And I said for her not to worry because you and I had built this trust between us and you'd never put me in any danger."

Magic stopped by the creek and nuzzled her arm.

"I'm right, aren't I?" she asked him.

He threw back his head as if to say, *"Totally. No question. One hundred percent."*

"So, that was it. I made my decision," she announced, looping her arms around Magic's neck. "Tomorrow we take on Becca and Pepper. We'll show the whole world what we can do!"

# Chapter 5

"Ta-da! We're back, you crazy, stunt-riding people!" Nathan Atwood burst into the dining room while everyone was eating breakfast. All the girls swooned and sighed over their crispy bacon and eggs over easy as he made his way around the room high-fiving everyone and demanding to know when he would get to ride the cool black horse again.

"Dark bay," Hayley told him, seemingly the only one who was not lost for words at the appearance of the movie star. "Liberty's a dark bay. He's Jack's horse, so he's the guy to ask."

Coreen glided into the room behind him, but instead of saying hello, she kept her head down, busily checking text messages on her phone.

"They're back!" Kami echoed Nathan's words. "That means Brad Morley really does want to take a second look at us."

"There's the man himself," Alisa said, pointing

out the window to where the director stood in the yard with Matt, Jack, and Lizzie.

"What happens now?" Kami whispered. She felt her stomach twist into a knot.

"It looks like Lizzie is definitely setting up more auditions," Kellie said as Jack headed toward the ranch house.

"Okay, Kami, get ready to impress. I'm sure they'll want to see you," Hayley predicted. "I wonder who they'll choose to double up for Nathan."

The knot in Kami's stomach grew even tighter. But she'd sworn to Magic last night that she would give this her best shot, and that was what she planned to do — if Lizzie put her up for the audition. And that was a big "if."

As Jack came into the dining room, everyone turned and held their breath. He looked around at their faces — some eager and excited, some nervous, and some resigned to the fact that they weren't even in the running. "Good news," he announced. "Thanks to my buddy Matt, we have a real chance of sealing the *Moonlight Dream* deal. Brad didn't find anyone to fit the bill at High Noon, so now he's back here for official auditions. He wants to see two possible contenders for Coreen's stunt double and two for Nathan's."

"Good job!" a couple of kids called out.

"Lizzie and I have decided who we want to

put forward." Jack let the tension mount, speaking slowly and walking between the tables until he got a good view of everyone gathered there. "The two boys who will be auditioning today are . . ."

Kami groaned inwardly. Jeez, this was worse than the *American Idol* results!

". . . Ross and Tom!" Jack declared.

There were whoops and cheers as the two boys stood up, ready to go out and saddle up their horses.

"And the two girls are . . ."

Kami gripped the edge of the table until her knuckles turned white. She swallowed hard.

". . . Becca and Kami!"

"Go, Becca! Go, Kami!" There were encouraging cheers, and some of the kids banged the tables with their utensils.

The noise almost deafened Kami as she stood up. Hayley grinned, and Alisa and Kellie nodded their support. "You can do it!" they mouthed.

Across the room, Kami watched Becca push her chair back. Her rival brimmed with confidence as she high-fived her neighbor, then went up to Coreen. "Come and watch," Becca said to the movie star as if they were already best buddies.

"Ready, Kami?" Jack called above the noise and general excitement. "Let's go."

Kami's legs wobbled as she crossed the room,

and by the time she reached the porch, she felt totally light-headed. But it was now or never, so setting her wide-brimmed straw Stetson low on her forehead to block the bright sun, she strode toward the corral.

∽ ◦ ൮

"This is it!" Kami told Magic as she brushed every last speck of dirt out of his coat and each tiny tangle out of his mane and tail.

Magic stood with his ears perked up, his attention fixed on Tom and Legend as they rode around the pen. Ross followed behind on his horse, Jack D, or Dee for short — a light sorrel the color of the famous whiskey.

Kami grinned. "I know," she said. "You want to get out there so you can see how they do. I'm working as fast as I can."

At the railing next to theirs, Becca had already tightened Pepper's cinch and was checking the length of her stirrups. By the entrance to the pen, Brad stood chatting with Matt and Jack, while Lizzie instructed the boys on the stunts she wanted them to perform.

"Okay, time to get your saddle on," Kami told Magic. She heaved the heavy tack into position, then fastened the girth loosely. "Now for your bridle."

Magic lowered his head as Kami slid the bit between his teeth. He stood patiently as she adjusted the straps.

"Ready?" Kami asked as she patted his forelock down over the brow band.

Magic gave a low snort and stamped his foot impatiently.

Beside them, Becca swung nimbly into her saddle. "Let's rock this," she told Pepper.

"Uh-oh, cinch," Kami muttered to herself, remembering to stoop and make the final check. She tightened the thick strap under Magic's belly by a couple of holes before she was satisfied. "Okay, now we're all set. Let's go."

∽ ◦ ∾

Ross was up first.

"We want to see Dee rear up and paw the air," Lizzie told him. "After that, we want him to crowhop across the pen, going into a full bucking session over by the far railing. You got that?"

Ross nodded. He looked relaxed in front of his audience, leaning forward to pat Dee. He walked his horse a full lap before he began the stunts.

"I'm not sure we want a plain brown horse," Brad muttered uncertainly to Matt and Jack. "Aren't they a little boring?"

"Dee has plenty of character," Jack explained. "Just you watch!"

With a subtle shift of weight, Ross asked his horse to rear up on his hind legs. The little sorrel pawed the air, his chestnut mane flinging back. Then he was down and arching his back, bouncing up from the ground off all four legs, while Ross raised his hat and waved it in the air like an old-time rodeo cowboy.

"Crowhopping," Jack informed the director. "And now bucking."

Ross used new pressure to make Dee plunge his head down and kick his back legs out. He rocked back as Dee landed, then forward again as the spirited sorrel threw in an extra buck.

"Whoa!" Lizzie called the display to a halt. "Thanks, Ross — good job. Now Tom — your turn."

Kami waited with Magic by the gate and watched Tom make a last adjustment to his stirrups as he took instructions from Lizzie. Legend looked great. Palominos were such pretty horses, with their honey-colored coats and blond manes and tails. She was sure Brad would be impressed. *Tom looks great in the saddle, too,* she thought with a blush.

"Tom will start with a front wing," Lizzie told the director. "That means he hangs onto the saddle horn with one hand, throws himself out of the saddle, and flings himself forward. Keep an eye on Legend — a strength of hers is her stamina."

Brad nodded. "I need these horses to race along a beach for a big scene in the movie," he noted. "Stamina would be good."

As Tom set Legend off at a canter, then flung himself forward out of the saddle, Kami noticed the work the horse was putting in, holding her balance and keeping up her pace as her rider threw himself around. She saw patches of sweat appear on her neck, but still Legend cantered on.

"Okay, Tom, finish with a double vault," Lizzie called.

Lizzie's words were barely out when Tom vaulted out of the saddle to one side, then back up again and out to the other. Finally, he vaulted into the saddle and reined his horse to a halt. Meanwhile, Lizzie got Becca and Pepper ready for their audition.

"Becca, I want you to show Brad some Roman riding. Kami, that means you'll ride Magic alongside Pepper and be prepared for Becca to stand and transfer her weight so that she straddles both horses. You got that?"

Kami nodded and eased Magic into position.

"Don't mess this up," Becca warned quietly.

"We won't," Kami promised. Other kids might

have been tempted to, but not her. She wanted this to be a fair competition, no dirty tricks.

The two riders set off side by side, their horses keeping perfect time.

"Good boy, Magic," Kami whispered as she sat quietly in the saddle while Becca stood nimbly on Pepper's back. Becca stood with arms stretched wide, bending her legs to absorb her horse's movement. When she stepped across to straddle the two horses and Magic felt her weight on his rump, he didn't falter. "Good, good boy!"

"Thanks, Kami! Thanks, Becca!" Lizzie called. When the stunt was complete and Becca was back on her own horse, she called Kami and Magic back to the gate while Becca finished off her display with a couple of vertical wings and a final dramatic saddle fall.

"And last but not least, Kami and Magic," Lizzie told Brad, while both Nathan and Coreen congratulated Becca on her audition.

"Is this the kid we saw yesterday, when we first got here?" the puzzled director asked Matt, looking from Kami to Becca and back again.

Tom, who was standing nearby, shot in with an answer. "Yeah, Kami and Magic — that's who you saw," he confirmed.

Kami smiled her thanks and tried not to tighten up. *Shoulders down, breathe easy, relax.*

"Let's see a few vaults," Lizzie told her. "Any sequence you like. Then spin the horn and vault out of the saddle to finish."

*Okay, we can do this!* Kami thought. She gathered her courage and felt Magic eager to go. Stepping out of the saddle, she clicked her tongue and set him off at a canter, clockwise around the pen. He circled once, and as he passed her, his nostrils flared and his nearside ear flicked toward her, she sprinted after him and with one bound, vaulted into the saddle.

Magic flicked both ears back toward her and trotted on.

Kami felt his strength, his smoothness, his total confidence. This horse lived up to his name. He was magic, and he would never let her down. She forgot the onlookers and began to enjoy herself — out of the saddle and running alongside, back up again with more strength in her arms and legs than she ever knew she had. Out again on the far side and sprinting, laughing as she vaulted back into the saddle.

Magic didn't falter or make one unsteady step. He and his new stunt rider were as one.

"Ready for our finale?" Kami whispered to him. "Spin the horn."

For this — the most difficult stunt — she put her weight forward onto the hand resting on the saddle horn, then alternated hands as she twisted her legs across Magic's back and over his neck until she'd turned full circle.

"Again!" she told him, adding an even faster spin. "And one last time." At the end of the third spin, she vaulted.

Magic slowed down and let her jog beside him. They came to a halt in front of the director and his two young stars.

"Good job, everyone," the director said. "You kids are definitely the best stunt riders we've seen so far. But now for the hard part." Brad didn't waste time when it came to casting decisions. He turned first to Ross and Jack D. "Son, I like the way you ride, and I'll keep you on my list for future work, no doubt about it." Then he turned to Tom. "But you're the same height as Nathan and the same build, plus Lizzie assures me your horse has enough stamina to race along the beach for however many takes we need."

"She sure does," Tom said, looping an affectionate arm around Legend's neck.

"So you get the job as Nathan Atwood's stunt double," Brad decided.

"Hey, partner!" Nathan gave Tom a high five, then told Ross he was an awesome rider anyway. "Another time, dude," he said.

Meanwhile, it was time for Brad's next choice.

"Now for the girls. This sure is hard," he admitted, looking down to check his notes.

Kami took a deep breath, then held it. Becca was smiling, looking super confident.

"Becca, your resumé is impressive — all your past work, your current level of skill. And Kami, you're new, so your record is unproven . . ."

Kami's heart sank. Brad would go for experience, for Becca's proven track record.

"However, that's not a problem," the director continued. "You're both excellent riders. So my decision here rests on one issue." He paused. "Let me ask you, Lizzie. We have three scenes to shoot on an open beach, so which one of these horses will work best in that situation?"

Lizzie looked from Magic to Pepper, then back again. Kami still held her breath.

"That would be Magic," Lizzie said slowly. "He's great around water."

Magic's ears perked up, as if he knew he was being praised. Becca turned away, trying to hide her disappointment.

Brad smiled and came forward to shake Kami's hand. "Then the job of Coreen Kessler's stunt double goes to you and Magic," he confirmed. "Pack your bags — you're flying out to California the day after tomorrow!"

# Chapter 6

Kami hardly knew that Sunday had happened.

She remembered calling home with the good news and her dad yelling for her mom to come to the phone to hear the words straight from Kami's mouth. "Heather, Kami's going to California!" She'd heard him shout out across the yard where new guests were arriving at Elk Creek. "Our daughter got a stunt-riding job!"

The rest of the day was a blur of laundry and packing, hanging out with Hayley, Kellie, and Alisa, taking apples to Magic in the meadow, and listening to last-minute instructions from Lizzie.

"Jack will fly out to Santa Barbara with you," she'd explained. "The horses will travel on the same plane — all at the movie company's expense. Don't look so worried. Our horses are used to plane trips, and there's no time to trailer them all the way to California."

Kami had been too excited to take in any

details, but she could see the relief in Lizzie's face as she and Jack discussed the finer details of the plans.

"Happy?" Tom asked her as he joined her in the laundry room with a ton of last-minute washing. "You went up against Becca and won."

"Don't I know it," Kami said. "She hasn't said a word to me since."

"Don't worry about Becca," Tom reassured her. "The important thing is, are you happy?"

"I'm more scared than happy," she admitted. "This is such a big deal."

Dropping his dirty laundry on the floor, Tom took Kami's hand and dragged her over to the soda machine, where they both sat down under the yellow umbrella. "So what's scaring you?" he asked.

"Everything," she said. The distance they had to travel, meeting the film crew, not making a fool of herself by messing up the stunts . . . Yeah, everything!

"Are you sitting here wondering if you can do this?" Tom guessed. The twinkle didn't leave his eyes as he shrugged and said, "Me, too."

"No — really?" Kami didn't believe him. "You've done this a dozen times."

"And each time I'm more scared than the time before, believe me," he admitted.

"No!" He was only saying this to help her.

"Yeah," he said as he leaned forward, elbows on the table, cradling his drink between his hands. "But you know what I do? I focus on Legend. I think about her and nothing else."

Kami listened carefully and found immediately that this made sense. *Concentrate on Magic and make sure he's happy,* she told herself.

"Thanks. That's good advice," she said to Tom, and she went out to the meadow to take another apple to her horse.

∾ ◦ ℃

At five-thirty on Monday morning, Lizzie came into Kami and Alisa's bedroom and quietly shook Kami awake.

Kami opened her eyes in the darkness. For a few seconds, she was confused.

"It's me," Lizzie said. "Time to go down to the meadow and bring Magic into the corral. Tom's already up and dressed."

The idea of Tom being ready before her got Kami out of bed. She quickly dressed in jeans and a T-shirt and was on her way outside in a flash. Her boots crunched on the gravel path as she zipped her jacket and glanced up at the mountainous horizon, where a pink gleam told her that the sun was slowly rising. Still, it was too dark to make out Tom's figure as he emerged from the barn.

"I got two halters," he called to her when he heard her coming. When she got close, he handed one to her, and they walked on in silence until they came to the meadow gate. "That's weird," Tom muttered, placing his hand on the gate and finding that it had swung open. "Someone left it unbolted."

Kami couldn't see much, but she could hear horses not far away, swishing their hooves through the grass as they approached or noisily grazing. "Everything seems fine," she said.

"No, it's definitely weird," Tom said. He stooped to examine the bolt. "Zak was the last person out here yesterday night — he drove the tractor loaded with alfalfa. No way would he forget to bolt the gate."

"Yeah, that is strange," Kami agreed. Then she clicked her tongue and raised her voice to call for Magic.

She expected him to nicker and come trotting up as usual, but he didn't this morning. She clicked, called again, and waited.

A horse appeared out of the pre-dawn gloom, but it was Cool Kid, not Magic — she recognized him by his brown-and-white markings, which showed clearly in the half-light. He came and nudged her uneasily with his nose, ears flattened and nostrils flared. "You're right. Something weird has happened," she said as alarm bells rang in her head.

"Yeah, and no sign of Legend." Tom strode across the meadow, halter in hand. "This is not good," he muttered.

"Magic, where are you?" Kami called as Cool Kid came up and nudged her back toward the gate. Today of all days was not the time for the horses to go missing.

Insistently, the little Paint pushed her back through the gate while Tom called for Kami to look up toward the dirt path leading out of the steep-sided valley. "I hear a truck!" he yelled.

"I can't see anything!" she yelled back, but just then a car's headlights raked across the hillside and the truck itself emerged from a stand of pine trees. Tom sprinted to join her just as the driver skidded around a final bend before vanishing out of sight.

"Jeez!" he groaned. "I didn't think even *he* would play such a dirty trick."

"What are you talking about?" Kami asked, worried.

"I recognize the truck," Tom muttered. "We just had an unscheduled visit from Pete Mason."

"Lizzie's ex?"

"Yep," Tom said. "He clearly doesn't like the fact that Lizzie and Jack won the *Moonlight Dream* contract. This must be his way of getting back at them."

"By opening the gate and letting our horses out?" Kami asked, not able to believe it. It took Kami some time to figure it out, but when she did, she felt a flash of anger mixed with panic. "How stupid is that! Doesn't he know it's dangerous for horses out there in the mountains!" she cried.

"Sure, he knows," Tom said grimly. "That's why he did it. It's going to be difficult to prove, though. It's our word against his."

"So why are we standing here talking?" Kami asked. She had no idea how many Stardust horses had escaped, and it was still too dark to count. What she did know was that Magic and Legend were definitely among those missing. "You go tell Lizzie and Jack what's happened. I'll ride around and start looking."

There was no time to lose. The sun was creeping over the horizon and hitting the mountaintops on the west side of the valley. Kami eased the halter onto Cool Kid and turned the lead rope into a rough version of reins. There was no bit in his mouth, but at least she had a little control as she vaulted onto his back and headed out toward the creek.

"Search in the willows!" Tom called after her as he ran to the ranch house. "And don't worry — horses see better in the dark than we do!"

"Okay, Cool Kid, you know what we have to do," Kami whispered, easing the horse into a canter along the bank. "We're looking for Legend and Magic and whoever else happens to be out here."

Hayley's plucky horse picked up speed, heading along the creek until they came to the island — the girls' favorite picnic spot. Here he slowed to a walk, then raised his head to give a shrill whinny.

Silence. There was no reply from the runaway horses.

"I don't know about you, Cool Kid, but I'm thinking bad things," Kami admitted. "I'm picturing coyotes and mountain lions."

She knew from experience at Elk Creek that coyotes hunted in packs, creeping silently through shadows, tracking their prey. Mountain lions were solitary hunters with sharp claws and powerful jaws. And they were active in the pre-dawn, stalking along the ridges, seeking out vulnerable victims — a sick calf, a wounded deer. She imagined Magic, perhaps injured and trapped in a narrow gorge, unable to escape.

Picking up on the urgency of his rider's voice,

Cool Kid raised his head again and listened intently.

Kami heard the wind in the trees, nothing else.

But the horse had picked up something. He turned away from the creek and sure-footedly set off up the mountain, crunching through loose gravel and across smooth granite rock until he came to a flat ledge and whinnied again.

This time Kami picked up a reply from higher up on the slope. It was faint, but it was definitely a horse answering Cool Kid's call.

"Good job — let's go!" she said, squeezing the horse's sides and letting him move toward a thick stand of pine trees.

A horse whinnied as they approached the trees, but the cry was drowned out by the howl of a coyote, then another and another. The sounds sent a chill down Kami's spine.

That horse could be hurt. He could easily have broken a leg out here! She pictured the pack of wild dogs crouching low, ready to pounce.

Kami and Cool Kid entered the stand of pines. A cold wind rustled the pine needles and made the branches creak. More coyotes joined in the chilling chorus. Kami leaned forward to pat the nervous horse's neck and urge him on.

At last they came to the entrance to a narrow ravine where rocks rose on either side. Cool Kid whinnied, and this time there was an answer from two or three different horses.

"Good boy!" Kami murmured, peering down into the dark ravine on the lookout for the pack of gray, silent hunters blocking the exit. Then she raised her voice. "Magic, are you in there?"

There was a high, familiar whinny, and at the same time, the first shaft of sunlight hit the ridge to the west.

There they were — five or six coyotes lined up with hackles raised, staring down into the ravine. Then they spotted Kami and Cool Kid.

"Yah!" Kami yelled a warning at the top of her voice, dropping Cool Kid's lead rope and waving both hands above her head. At the same time, a pale shape emerged from the gloom, followed by two others. "Magic, thank goodness you're safe!" Recognizing the lead horse, Kami slipped from Cool Kid's back and ran toward him.

Up on the ridge, the disappointed coyotes began to retreat. First one, then another slipped out of view.

"It's okay. Everything's okay!" Kami greeted Magic as Legend and Pepper followed him out of the gully. Right away, Kami saw that Pepper was limping. "Good boy, you took care of Pepper," she whispered in Magic's ear. "You were scared of the coyotes, but you didn't leave him. Good, brave boy! And you, too, Legend. What happened to you, Pepper?"

Becca's horse was in so much pain that he was hardly able to put any weight on the injured leg, and Kami could see there was already swelling on the knee joint. He was trembling, and his neck and belly were covered in sweat. "It's okay," she said soothingly. "The coyotes are gone. Now we need to get you back home fast."

But how to get four horses down the mountain and back to the safety of the corral without any ropes or other tack? She needed help and hoped that Tom was bringing Jack and Lizzie in the right direction. "They'll follow our tracks," she told Cool Kid, sounding more certain than she felt.

The horses stood, heads raised. With one hand on Magic's neck, Kami strained to hear.

Silence . . . then came a distant whinny from down in the valley, answered by Cool Kid, the hero of the hour. He whinnied a second time, and soon Magic and Legend joined in.

"It won't be long," Kami promised Pepper, as the horse trembled with pain. Her mind was racing now, thinking ahead. Even if they got everyone safely back to Stardust, would there still be time to get Magic and Legend loaded on the trailer, ready to fly them out to California?

*If not, Pete Mason will get exactly what he wanted,*

she thought. *He'll have wrecked the whole* Moonlight Dream *deal!*

She waited and watched. Every moving shadow fooled her into thinking that help had arrived, but the minutes ticked by as the sun rose higher in the sky.

"Hurry!" she urged.

At last! Jack and Liberty were the first to appear. Kami saw the look of relief on Jack's face as he spotted them at the entrance to the ravine. "Stay right where you are," he called to Kami. "We'll be with you in five minutes."

"You hear that, Pepper?" Kami whispered to the injured horse.

Becca's horse took three limping steps down the slope toward Jack, then stopped.

"She's lame," Kami called down to Jack. "There was a pack of coyotes after them. I'm guessing her foot got caught in a crack and she twisted her knee."

"Keep her right there," Jack instructed again as Tom appeared behind him riding Dylan, followed by Lizzie on Sugar. "And Kami, block the exit so the others can't take off again."

She did as Jack told her, and soon he and Liberty made it up the mountain with halters for the runaways. By the time Lizzie and Tom had joined him, all the horses were secure and Jack was running his hands over Pepper's swollen knee.

Now it was Lizzie's turn to make decisions. "Tom, you grab Legend's lead rope and take her down the mountain while you ride Dylan. Kami, you ride Cool Kid and lead Magic home. Jack, I'll ride on ahead of Tom and Kami and drive the small trailer up the Jeep path to meet you, Liberty, and Pepper at Snake Rock. I think it's about six hundred feet north of here. Do you think Pepper can make it that far?"

"I guess so," Jack said. He quickly checked his watch. "We have one hour to get Magic and Legend ready to trailer out to the airport," he reminded Tom and Kami. "Can we do it?"

"You bet!" they told him. No way was Pete Mason's sabotage going to stop them from getting to the *Moonlight Dream* film set on time and prepared.

# Chapter 7

It was only when Kami had Magic safely tethered to a railing in the corral that she finally breathed easy.

The journey down the mountain had gone well. There had been no problem leading Legend and Magic back to the stables. By the time the corral was in sight, Tom and Kami could see that Lizzie had already jumped into the small trailer to drive back up to Snake Rock. Still, Kami hadn't relaxed until she and Cool Kid had led Magic along the creek and into the yard.

"Hey, Kami!" Hayley ran out of the ranch house to take Cool Kid from her. "We heard what happened. Is everyone okay?"

Kami nodded. "Your horse was amazing," she said. "He tracked down the runaways."

"You bet he did!" Hayley said with a smile. "Cool Kid, you're so smart!" she cooed as she tied him to a nearby railing and brushed him down.

Kellie had already taken Dylan from Tom and left him to deal with Legend. "You two need to work fast," she reminded them.

"Thanks for telling me something I already knew, Sis," Tom replied.

"Did someone call the vet for Pepper?" Kami asked as she started to groom Magic.

"Becca's on it right now," Kellie answered.

As she spoke, Becca appeared on the ranch house porch, shading her eyes against the low morning sun. She seemed nervous and held back from joining the group as she glanced anxiously in the direction of Snake Rock.

"So we heard Pete Mason paid us a visit," Hayley commented.

Tom nodded and said, "It looks like he went into the meadow and deliberately separated Legend and Magic from the rest, then spooked them so bad they took off into the mountains. Pepper probably got mixed up in the drama by accident."

Kellie frowned as she watched Becca slowly step down from the porch. "Maybe this is me being too suspicious," she began, "but you don't think —"

"That Becca was involved?" Hayley broke in. "Why would she be?"

"Maybe she was so jealous that she wanted to

wreck the new deal. Maybe she called Mason and put the idea in his head," Kellie suggested.

But Hayley didn't sound convinced. "No way!" she said. "Becca wouldn't risk her own horse!"

"Not on purpose," Kellie pointed out. "But what if Tom's right and Pepper got involved accidentally?"

Becca was now too close to the corral for them to share any more suspicions.

As Kami ran her brush through Magic's mane, she wondered if her rival was ruthless enough to try something like that. But she quickly banished the thought from her mind.

"Hey, Becca." Kellie's tone was curt. "Have you talked to the vet?"

Becca walked slowly into the corral and across to the tack-room porch, where she stood in the shade. "He's on his way," she confirmed.

Kami sneaked a look over Magic's shoulder. Becca was drained of her normal confidence; she looked all shaken up. "Try not to stress. Pepper will be back soon," Kami called.

"Thanks," Becca said. She glanced at her watch, then hung her head. She seemed to think for a while, then came over and hovered close to Kami, all the time searching the Jeep path for signs of the returning trailer.

Kami reached for the protective tail bandage

that Magic would wear for the long journey out to Santa Barbara. Slowly and methodically, she began to bind his tail.

"So, Pepper's lame?" Becca began quietly.

Kami nodded. "It looks like he sprained the ligaments in his knee."

"But it's not too bad?" Becca asked, her voice breaking.

Kami glanced up to see tears in Becca's eyes. "Like Jack said, fingers crossed it's nothing too serious," she reassured her. "Maybe painkillers and rest for a couple of days."

"I feel so lousy," Becca mumbled.

Kami felt the tension in the corral mount. Hayley, Kellie, and Tom were all listening to their conversation.

"What have you got to feel bad about?" Kellie asked pointedly.

There was a long pause while Becca gulped back tears. "For not being there for Pepper when he needed me," she said. "It should have been me riding out to find him, not Kami."

Kami almost heard the sighs of relief from the others. "Don't beat yourself up," she consoled Becca. "Your horse is sure going to need all the love you can give him when he gets back to Stardust."

"I'll be there for him twenty-four seven," Becca

said. Her eyebrows furrowed as she thought for a while. Then she finally asked, "So, how did they get out of the meadow in the first place?"

"You didn't hear about Pete Mason?" Kami asked.

Becca frowned in genuine puzzlement. "No — what about him?"

"Me and Tom, we saw him heading out of here just before dawn."

"Driving like a crazy guy," Tom confirmed without looking up or breaking the rhythm of his brushstrokes through Legend's blond mane. "Our theory is that he was the one who unbolted the gate and drove Magic and Legend out to the mountain. We think Pepper got involved because he was in the wrong place at the wrong time."

Becca shook her head and groaned. "That lousy, low-down . . ."

"Exactly," Kami agreed. She finished Magic's tail bandage and reached for the padded boots to protect his legs.

"We have to tell the cops," Becca spoke rapidly. "Our horses could've died. The guy should go to jail for this."

If there was still any lingering doubt in anyone's mind, Becca's flushed, angry face would have convinced them. No way was she faking it.

Kami nodded, then bent down to strap on

Magic's boots. "Easy, boy," she murmured as he shifted his weight.

"Leave it to me," Becca told her, realizing that Kami and Tom were racing against time. "I'll talk it through with Lizzie, and we'll make sure Pete Mason doesn't get away with this." She spotted Lizzie driving the trailer back down and hurried off to meet her. When she reached the corral gate, she hesitated and retraced her steps. "One more thing," she whispered to Kami.

Kami looked up from under Magic's arched neck.

"Thank you for finding Pepper," Becca said.

"Honestly, it was nothing," Kami replied.

"No, really, Kami — thank you." Becca's face was flushed, her eyes full of tears again. "And I want to say sorry."

"For what?" Standing up straight, Kami looked Becca in the eye.

"For acting the way I did," Becca mumbled. "For . . . you know, for being jealous and not making you feel welcome here at Stardust. For being mean to you during the tryouts."

"No problem. Really." Now it was Kami's turn to feel hot and flushed. "We both really wanted that job."

"So, that's it — thank you and sorry," Becca insisted. "Are we friends?"

"Friends," Kami said slowly. She smiled, then grabbed Becca's arm and turned her back toward the Jeep path. "Go!" she insisted.

Becca nodded, then sprinted for the gate.

Kami took a deep breath. *Wow, that was a big surprise,* she thought with a long, satisfied sigh. *Now all I have to do is get on that plane and prove to Brad Morley that he made the right choice when he picked me as Coreen Kessler's stunt double!*

∽ ◦ ℃

Flying over the Rockies at 32,000 feet, Kami gazed down on endless miles of gray mountains broken up by dark patches of forest and thin silver rivers snaking through. From up in the air, it looked like vast and hostile land.

"It makes you wonder how people ever made it through to the west coast," she said to Tom.

"A lot died trying," he said. He tilted his seat back, stretching his long legs into the aisle.

"Do you want to switch seats so you can take a look out the window?" Kami offered.

"No, thanks. I just want to get there," he said.

"Me too," Kami admitted. "How do you think Magic and Legend are doing down there?"

"They'll be just fine," Tom assured her. "Remember, this is a special equine aircraft — the stalls in there are air-conditioned, and Jack's with them."

It had been a close call — the drive to Denver International, the paperwork checks, the loading of the horses into the hold, the hurried check-in at the departure gate, making it through security with only minutes to spare. But they'd made it onto the Santa Barbara flight, and their estimated arrival time was 3:20 p.m.

"Chill," Tom advised Kami, who was fiddling with her air-conditioning control switch. "Get some beauty sleep."

"I can't sleep on planes," she said, sighing. "Hey, what do you mean 'beauty sleep'? Are you saying I need it?"

Tom laughed. "No, you look fine, believe me — except for the bags under your eyes . . ." he said. "Ha, joke! All I'm saying is, you'll want to look your best now that you get to work on set with the world's hottest screen idol."

"Nathan Atwood?" Kami asked.

"Who else? I saw you when he came into the ranch house that first day. You were drooling over him just like the rest of the girls," Tom said.

"I was not!" Kami protested.

"Were," Tom replied.

"Was not. Anyway, what about you and Coreen Kessler?" Kami teased.

"Not my type," he lied.

"Oh, c'mon!" Kami said. "You don't fool me, Coreen is everybody's type. You're telling me that you alone — out of all the boys I know — wouldn't kill to date her?"

Raising his eyebrows and giving a small shrug, Tom plugged in his earphones and tuned into the on-board movie. "Hey, guess who's starring!" he said, pointing to the screen at a close-up shot of a moody-looking Nathan Atwood playing a vampire in his latest blockbuster release. "It's your crush!"

Kami groaned and closed her eyes. It was going to be a long trip.

∽ ◦ ℘

They had to do more paperwork when they arrived in California, which meant more hanging around for Jack, Kami, and Tom. It was late afternoon by the time they drove Magic and Legend out of Santa Barbara's airport and headed south along the coast.

"So, where are we going now?" Tom asked Jack, whose black shirt and Stetson looked out of place in the urban sprawl.

"The film crew is based at a ranch called Five Sisters, twenty miles outside of town," Jack said as he negotiated traffic lights and followed signs for Highway 61. "The ranch is backed by a National Forest wilderness area and looks out on the Pacific Ocean."

"Is that where we'll do the beach scenes?" Kami asked.

"Yep. And you're about to get thrown into the deep end — excuse the pun," Jack told her. "Tomorrow Brad wants to shoot a big scene where Coreen's character rides her horse along the beach. It climaxes with the girl falling from her horse and getting dragged along the sand."

"Simple," Tom assured Kami. "Saddle fall followed by a drag. You can do that, no problem."

Tom was confident in her abilities, but Kami frowned as she stared at the road ahead. It seemed like just yesterday that she'd been a normal kid living on a guest ranch, riding her horse along mountain trails. Now here she was in sunny California, driving out to a movie set, discussing complicated stunts, and committed to working in front of cameras and crew with actors she'd only ever seen and read about in magazines. Crazy!

"You're quiet, Kami," Jack said. "Are you okay?"

"I'm good," she muttered. The sun was quickly sinking over the ocean to their right, and Kami watched the tiny figures of surfers riding the crests of waves before they crashed onto the shore. She saw miles of empty white beach ahead. "I just hope I don't let you and Lizzie down."

"You won't," Jack promised. "Just trust Magic. Listen to what he says."

∽ ◦ ⌒

"Okay, Magic, this is home for the next few days."

The journey was over and Kami was introducing her horse to where he'd be staying at Five Sisters Ranch, a sprawling, Spanish-style set-up with white stucco buildings and red-tiled roofs.

Magic stood at the gate, looking out onto a meadow where Legend was already grazing.

"I know — the grass isn't as green and lush as you're used to. It's hot here in the summer, and they don't get lots of rain. But you'll get alfalfa morning and night," Kami promised.

Magic took a couple of steps into the small meadow with its white fences and fancy metal feeder. He glanced up at the forested hillside beyond.

"Los Padres National Forest," Kami explained. "And that sound you hear in the distance? That's the Pacific Ocean."

Still, Magic hesitated, reluctant to follow Legend across the meadow.

"Go!" Kami told him as he nuzzled her arm.

Magic tilted his head, then nuzzled her again, as if checking that she was certain.

"Sure!" she insisted breezily. It was dusk, but it was still warm enough to wear only a T-shirt and jeans. As Magic finally sauntered off to join Legend, Kami bolted the gate and walked back toward the ranch house, past giant trucks loaded with film equipment, and silver trailers and SUVs, which housed the crew. A bright lamp cast yellow light on the main porch. Kami picked out Tom and Jack talking with Matt, then Brad with a couple of older guys, and finally, standing to one side, the unmistakable figures of Coreen and Nathan.

"Kami?" Nathan was the first to spot her as she halted by the last of the SUVs, and he gestured for her to join them. "You remember me, right?"

Swallowing hard, Kami stepped up into the porch and nodded. "How could I not?"

"Yeah, I guess," Nathan said. He grinned. "Sorry — I'm still not used to being famous. Listen, you and Coreen need to talk."

"We do?" Kami asked.

"You definitely do. But don't tell Brad — okay?"

"Okay," Kami agreed uncertainly. She was

instantly feeling unfriendly vibes radiating from Coreen.

"Leave it, Nathan," Coreen snapped. "That was a private conversation between you and me."

"My mistake," he said. He shrugged and gave Kami an apologetic smile as Coreen turned on her heel and disappeared into the house. "Prima donna!" he whispered, cupping his hand around his mouth.

Kami smiled. *Who could resist those big brown eyes? Deep breath, be cool.* "Will you be on . . . uh . . . set tomorrow?" she asked, tripping over her words and blushing. So not cool!

"Yeah, I just checked my schedule," Nathan replied, giving her that great smile again. Kami blushed even more.

"It's my first-ever shoot," she mumbled, then babbled on. "I guess you already knew that." *As if he cares,* she told herself with a sigh. *He's Nathan Atwood!*

He smiled — oh, that smile!

"So, Kami, I have to go. They need me in the wardrobe trailer. But I'll be on the beach at eight-thirty," he said. "See you there!"

# Chapter 8

Kami read the script five times before breakfast. She studied the scenes before and after the one of her galloping along the beach. She looked at the schedule to triple-check her eight a.m. start.

"Jittery?" Jack asked as she went out to fetch Magic from the meadow at six-thirty. He and Tom were already there, loading hay into the feeder.

"Yeah," she said. In fact, Kami had tossed and turned most of the night, rehearsing in her mind the moment on the beach when she would fling herself sideways from Magic's back, leaving one foot in the stirrup and allowing herself to be dragged along the ground for sixty feet. As usual, it would cost her a few bruises. Plus, it would need split-second timing and total understanding between her and her horse.

"It's good to be nervous," Jack insisted. "You wouldn't be human otherwise."

Nodding, she buckled Magic's halter and led

him into a small corral behind the row of silver trailers where the actors were getting ready for the morning's scenes. A moment later, Matt emerged from the wardrobe trailer, all buttoned up in a business suit, button-up shirt, and tie. He nodded at Coreen as she entered the makeup trailer next door, then came over to where Kami was grooming Magic.

"Did they give you your costume yet?" he asked.

Kami shook her head, then stood back to admire Magic's flowing dark mane and tail.

"They probably need you in the wardrobe trailer then — to check your dress size and everything."

"You're right — I better get over there!" said Kami, feeling a wave of nerves hit her. She spied Tom returning from the meadow and called for him to keep an eye on Magic. "Don't let him roll in the dirt," she said. "You hear that, Magic? No rolling!"

Her horse cocked his head to one side as if to say, *"Who, me?"*

Kami grinned and ran to be fitted for her costume.

Inside the trailer she met Wanda, the wardrobe stylist, who looked her up and down.

"You're Coreen's stunt double?" she asked.

Kami nodded. She felt excited that she was about to be dressed in the same clothes as Coreen.

"Take off your jeans and T-shirt," Wanda instructed, taking a long pale blue dress from the rack of costumes that ran the length of the trailer. "Try this. You look like you're the same dress size as Coreen, so it should fit pretty well."

Wow! Kami's hands trembled a little as she put on the sleeveless, close-fitting dress. Catching sight of herself in a full-length mirror, she saw that the cornflower shade of blue brought out the color of her eyes, and the shape flattered her slim figure.

"Like it?" Wanda asked.

She nodded.

"It looks good to me," said Wanda with a nod.

"Do I get shoes?" Kami asked, glancing down at her bare feet.

Wanda checked her list. "No shoes," she confirmed. "We're going for a romantic, shampoo-ad look." Then she took a couple of outfits from the rack, including a second pale blue dress. "Has anyone seen Coreen this morning?" she called through the open door. "I need her to get dressed."

"Still in makeup," a voice replied.

"Someone drag her out of there right away, and send her in here," Wanda insisted. "Brad's scheduled to start filming at seven. You know how he is when anyone keeps him waiting."

As a runner went to fetch Coreen, Kami stepped out of the trailer in her flowing blue dress, planning to go check on Magic one more time before Jack trailered him the short distance to the beach. Instead, she almost ran into Nathan, who sidestepped quickly and laughed at her for not looking where she was going.

"Hey, nice costume!" he added with a smile.

"Thanks," she said.

"So, where's the fire?" he asked.

"No fire." She bit her lip and tried not to say anything too stupid. "We're driving Magic down to the beach. You want to come?"

*Of course not,* she thought. *Why would drop-dead gorgeous Nathan Atwood want to drive with me in a smelly horse trailer?*

"Sure. Why not?" he said. Then he followed her to where Jack and Tom were already loading Magic into the trailer. "Hey, Tom, don't you need to be in costume, too?" he asked.

Tom didn't seem to want to stop and chat. "Not yet," he muttered as he tethered Magic to the railing inside the trailer.

"So when do I get to shoot my scene with the legendary Legend?" Nathan asked.

"That would be tomorrow," Tom told him, bolting the trailer door. "Today we get to chill."

"And you have to do all the work," Nathan

said to Kami as he stood aside and let her climb into the cab before him.

She sat in the middle seat, between Jack and Nathan, trying hard not to put creases in her dress.

Jack started the engine, then paused to lean out the driver's window and give some suggestions to Tom. "Why don't you saddle Legend and maybe ride her up into the forest? Just give her a gentle workout. Or else let her see the location on the beach where she'll be working tomorrow."

"Gotcha," Tom replied abruptly, glancing quickly at Nathan and Kami in the cab. "I sure wouldn't want to get in anyone's way."

*Oh, no!* Kami wanted to lean out and tell him, *"It's not like that. Nathan's way out of my league, just like Coreen is for you."* But she was too embarrassed to say anything.

Meanwhile, Nathan began to fill Kami in on some of the backstory to the scenes being filmed this morning. "This is where Krystal, Coreen's character, is in a big fight with her dad, played by Matt. She's trying to ride her horse on the beach when she should be in school. Mean Dad yells at her, saying he's going to sell the horse as punishment."

Kami nodded. "I read that part."

"Cool. Krystal goes crazy — no way is Mean

Dad going to sell her beloved horse. She runs to the stables and jumps in the saddle. Cue your out-of-control gallop along the beach, Kami," Nathan said.

By now, Jack had driven them into a low, forested headland and a parking lot filled with trucks containing cameras and sound equipment.

"You okay?" Jack checked with Kami as he looked for a spot to park the trailer.

*This is really happening!* Kami thought as she picked out Brad and Matt surrounded by crew. She took a deep breath.

"Sure, she's okay," Nathan answered for her as he opened the door and jumped down from the cab. He gave Kami a big smile and offered his hand for her to follow. "Dude, it's not Kami we have to worry about — it's Coreen."

Just then a silver SUV with shaded windows bumped along the path and came to a halt next to Magic's trailer.

"Here she is now," Nathan warned as the car door opened and the teen star stepped out, her long blond hair flowing in the breeze. She launched into a look-at-me strut. "Fasten your seat belts, guys. Enjoy the ride!" he said.

∽ ◦ ◠

"Action!"

Kami felt like she could reach out and touch the tension in the air as Brad's assistant director called for silence and the cameras rolled.

Matt stood beside the sand dunes that bordered the long strip of white beach. He eyeballed Coreen and yelled at her. Coreen yelled back — boy, was she good at yelling!

"Krystal, you don't have a choice — you have to stay in school and study!" Mean Dad yelled angrily at her.

"Why do I? School sucks. I'm going to get Moonlight from the stable, and you can't stop me!" Krystal retorted.

"Watch me," Mean Dad muttered, and the camera followed him as he strode toward a house overlooking the beach.

Krystal chased after him. "What are you doing?"

"What's it look like I'm doing? I'm going into the house, and I'm calling the dealer."

"The horse dealer?"

"You got it. Your precious Moonlight is going back to the sale barn, end of story," said Mean Dad, and he disappeared inside.

"Dad, wait!" Krystal began to run after him, but then she stopped suddenly. She paused uncertainly for a second before turning and running as fast as she could toward the stable at the side of the house.

"Cut!" Brad called. "Good work, everyone."

∽ ◦ ∾

It was now time for Jack to pace out Magic and Kami's action sequence. He explained the backstory as they walked. "Krystal has defied her dad by riding Moonlight along the shore, but her dad sticks with his plan to send the horse back to the sale barn," he said. "Early the next morning, he plans to load her horse into a trailer, only to find that Krystal's there first and Moonlight is already tacked up. Krystal fights with her dad, flings open the gate of the corral, and tells Moonlight to run for his life."

"That's where Magic and I come in?" Kami asked.

"Yep. Magic gallops to the shoreline, and then he stops and waits," Jack said, identifying a spot on the beach marked by a small yellow flag.

"You hear that?" Kami asked Magic. "You gallop to the flag, then you wait for me."

Magic breathed out through relaxed lips.

"Then, Kami, you run from the yard toward Magic. Don't worry about where the cameras are. Your job is to focus on Magic and do the stunt."

"Which side do I mount?"

"From the left," Jack told her. "Then, once you're in the saddle, rein Magic toward the ocean and launch into a canter."

"Canter." Kami repeated the instruction, internalizing every word Jack said.

"Pick up speed and gallop him into the water, through the breaking waves."

"Cool." Kami nodded and smiled at Magic. "You'll love that."

"About a hundred feet past the flag, a guy walking his dog will suddenly appear. They'll come out of the forest and across the dunes. The dog will run toward Magic and spook him."

"Spook," Kami echoed. "That's when Magic rears and tosses me out of the saddle?"

Jack nodded. "We need a saddle fall to the left followed by a left-foot drag."

"Got it," she said. Now that she'd walked it through with Jack and knew exactly what she had to do, Kami was ready for her stunt-riding debut. "Let's do it," she told Magic, leading him back to the yellow flag.

∽ ◦ ᕫ

"Action!" The director had his cameras in position. Magic had galloped across the white sand and stood at the water's edge while Kami waited in the stable yard.

She set off at a run, the wind blowing her hair from her face, salt from the ocean spray making her skin tingle. Her bare feet sank into the soft sand until she reached the water, where it was firmer. There she managed to pick up speed.

Magic stood patiently. He didn't flinch when Kami reached him and leaped into the saddle.

"Good boy," she whispered, kicking him lightly. She felt the strength of his hindquarters as he rocked back, then launched himself into a strong canter.

Getting into his stride, Magic picked up speed and galloped through the shallow, white-crested waves, kicking up spray that sparkled in the sun. Twenty feet, thirty feet galloping through the clear, shallow water, with endless turquoise ocean to the left, dunes and trees to the right. Fifty feet. Kami and Magic worked beautifully together. Eighty feet, a hundred . . . the man and dog appeared right on cue. The dog had been trained to bark and then run toward the horse, with the man helpless to stop him.

Magic and Kami both saw the lean, black dog. Kami gave her horse the signal to spook and rear, and within a split second, Magic broke his stride, twisted away from the dog, and raised himself onto his back legs. Kami was thrown off-balance so fast and hard that she lost her reins.

"Good boy!" she whispered again as Magic's front hooves landed close to the dog's head. The dog cringed and crept away, back to his master. Pressure from her left leg told Magic to wheel around to the right, again so hard and fast that it appeared Kami had lost her balance. She fell to her left, completely out of the saddle, keeping her foot hooked in the stirrup so that when Magic launched himself into another gallop, she was dragged through the shallow waves.

Ten, fifteen — Kami counted Magic's strides. *Thank goodness this is happening in water,* she thought. Water and soft sand cut down on the bruises at least. On the count of twenty she kicked herself free.

"Cut!" Brad yelled through his megaphone. "Terrific job, Kami. You're a natural!"

She was up on her feet, soaked to the bone, feeling her ribs ache a little as she took a deep breath. Magic slowed to a trot, then turned to come back to her. "Magic, you were more than terrific . . . you were totally perfect!" she said, throwing both her arms around his neck.

∽ ◦ ⌒

Back at Five Sisters and already changed out of her wet dress, Kami decided to give Magic a full pampering session. She took off his saddle, then brushed the sand out of his mane and tail. Then she hosed him down to get rid of the salt from the seawater.

"Feels good, huh?" she asked.

Lowering his head, Magic shook his whole body, swishing his tail and showering Nathan and Tom, who stood nearby.

"Sorry about that," Kami said, giggling.

Nathan laughed. "No, you're not."

"No, really!" Kami shrieked as Nathan made a grab for the hose and aimed it right at her. Kami ducked out of the way.

"Oops!" Nathan exclaimed as the jet of water hit Tom right in the chest. "Sorry, dude. Kami, what are you doing, putting your stunt-riding buddy in the line of fire?"

"It's cool," Tom muttered, but his body language said different. He turned his back on Nathan and Kami, lifted Legend's saddle from the railing, and carried it off to the barn without saying another word.

Kami frowned. She felt bad for Tom.

Nathan handed the hose back to Kami, and she finished rinsing Magic's belly and legs.

"Where were you earlier?" Kami asked Tom

when he came back, still dripping. "I didn't see you and Legend down at the beach."

Tom still refused to look at her as he shook his head. "We decided to ride through the forest instead."

"Dude, you missed Kami's debut," Nathan told him. "A new star was born."

"Magic was the star," Kami insisted as she turned off the hose. She walked him out to the meadow with Nathan still in tow. Looking over her shoulder, she noticed that Tom had walked off in the opposite direction.

"I mean it, Kami," Nathan insisted as she opened the gate and let Magic loose. "You're a great rider."

"Thanks," she said, "but I could never do what you and Coreen do in front of a camera — no way!"

"Are you kidding?" Nathan asked.

"No. Learning a script, remembering my lines, acting it out, and making it seem real . . . I couldn't do it. I mean, just look at the scene Coreen did this morning — the fight with her dad," Kami said.

"She's a good actress," Nathan acknowledged, then hesitated. "The best. It's just . . ."

Kami closed the gate, then leaned against it, giving Nathan a searching look. "Is this about the secret Coreen didn't want me to know?"

Nathan nodded. "There's a problem," he admitted. "She'll probably be super mad if she find out I told you this, but I — we need to do something."

"About what?" Kami asked, growing more and more curious.

"Let me ask you a question," he said. Pacing back and forth, Nathan glanced toward the catering trailer where the cast and crew had gathered for lunch. He spotted Coreen sitting at a table with Matt and Jack. "Have you noticed how Coreen acts around horses?"

Kami thought back to Nathan and Coreen's visits to the stables. "You mean when she first came to Stardust?" she asked.

"Yeah. Do you remember how she refused to ride the horse?" Nathan asked.

Still puzzled, Kami shrugged. "She was more interested in texting her friends, I guess."

"The texting stuff — it was a front," Nathan explained. "Just like the hair flicking and the head-in-the-air ignoring everyone."

"A front for what? What exactly is Coreen hiding?"

Nathan came to a halt right next to Kami and sighed. "You know how some people love horses and some are terrified of them? Or do you just figure everyone loves them as much as you do?"

"No, I get it. Horses are hundreds of pounds of solid muscle, and they're strong," said Kami. "Plus, their kicks can do a lot of damage."

"So they're unpredictable and dangerous?"

"Only if you don't know what to look out for," Kami replied.

"But people who are scared of horses *don't* know what to look out for — that's my point," Nathan explained. "I tried to speak to Coreen afterward, and she was shaking like a leaf. Her hands were trembling so much she could hardly use her phone."

"At the idea of riding a horse?" Kami said in a disbelieving tone.

Nathan nodded. "Or of going anywhere near one, actually."

Kami frowned and took a moment to think it through. "Will she need to do that?" she asked.

"Yeah, after you leave," Nathan explained. "There's a guy named Scott Maxwell who's in charge of the horses on this movie. His official title is Head Wrangler. Well, he found three horses identical to Magic to double as Moonlight in the scenes that don't involve any stunts. That's when Coreen has to get up close and personal with Moonlight to shoot the non-stunt-riding scenes."

"I didn't know that," Kami admitted. But it made sense — there would be scenes with Krystal and Moonlight in the stable, probably with lots of close-up camera shots that only Coreen could do.

"It happens all the time," he said. "You guys get to do the exciting stunts, but you're only on set for a week at most. You have to move on to work on something else, leaving us to do the boring stuff!"

Just then, Nathan saw his co-star get up from the table and start to walk in their direction with a frown on her face. He hurried to finish the explanation. "It's gotten worse since our first visit to Stardust. Coreen made up this story for Brad that she has an allergy. She says she gets asthma and breaks out in a rash whenever she goes near a horse, blah, blah, blah."

"So that she doesn't have to do any horse-related scenes?" Kami asked.

"Exactly," said Nathan. "But no way will Brad buy that. The focus of *Moonlight Dream* is Krystal's relationship with her horse and how the character I play helps save the horse from the sale barn. If she spins the allergy story, Brad will turn around and tell her to take some medicine for it. She'll have to do the scenes anyway. Otherwise, he'll fire her from the movie."

Kami glanced around. Coreen was heading their way. She was frowning and looking suspicious.

"You're saying that we need to solve Coreen's problem for her to stay in the role?" Kami asked.

"Bottom line is, can you make her love her horse?" Nathan pressed.

"How long do we have?" Kami asked.

"Until tomorrow morning, when Coreen shoots her first scene with Moonlight." Putting on a fake, reassuring smile, Nathan got ready to greet Coreen. "Can you do it?" he asked Kami out of the side of his mouth.

"I'll try," she decided, opening the gate to fetch Magic. "What do you say we start right now?"

# Chapter 9

"Nathan, how could you do this to me?" Coreen yelled. She stood with Nathan, Kami, and Magic in the small meadow behind the trailers. "It was our secret!"

"I only told Kami because I think she can help," he protested.

"I don't need help!" she said.

"Listen, Coreen, either you let Kami teach you how to make friends with horses, or you lose your job!" Nathan tried to reason with his co-star, but she was so angry that she didn't seem to care who else heard. "You have to learn not to be scared, that's all I'm saying."

"But you told . . . *her*!" With a dismissive flick of her hand, Coreen let Kami know that she wasn't worth talking to directly. "Nathan, she's a no-name stunt double. They can hire any one of ten girls to step in and do her job, and you have to make sure she understands that."

"Whoa!" he objected. "Kami's cool. You can trust her."

"Nathan was only trying to help," Kami said. She felt the sting of Coreen's insults, but she still stepped in to try to halt her meltdown. "And I'm not going to say anything. This is still a secret — believe me."

Coreen stepped back until she felt she was a safe distance from Kami and Magic. "Keep him away from me," she begged. "Look at his eyes. Honestly, I-I can't even stand the way they stare at me!"

Kami held tight to Magic's lead rope. She shook her head and stayed quiet because whatever she said or did only seemed to make things worse.

"He's still staring!" Coreen cried, covering her face with her hands. "I think I'm going to faint!"

"This isn't going to work," Kami whispered to Nathan.

"And now you're both talking behind my back and making fun of me!" cried Coreen.

Still holding her hands in front of her eyes, she wheeled around and began to run. As she reached the gate, she stumbled and almost collided with Jack, who'd come looking for Kami to see if she was ready for the afternoon's filming.

∽ ◦ ⌒

"You can only help someone who wants to be helped," Jack declared when Kami clammed up over the disaster that had occurred. "No need to break any promises," he told her. "Coreen was yelling at the top of her lungs, so I heard every word."

"I guess." Kami sighed. They'd reached the yard where the trailer was parked, so she lowered the ramp for Jack to lead Magic in. "Coreen said something that really hurt," she confessed quietly, smoothing down her long blue dress, which Wanda had dried and ironed during lunch. "She said I wasn't special . . . that a whole bunch of girls could step in and do my job."

"Not true," Jack said firmly as he loaded Magic and then came back down the ramp.

Kami smiled. "Thanks, Jack. But you're right, Coreen wasn't ready to listen to advice . . . especially not from me."

"Come on, get in the cab," he told her. "You tried to help; you did what you thought was right. Now you have to tell yourself it's not your problem."

Kami knew that what Jack said made sense, so she tried to focus on the scene scheduled for the afternoon. "This is where Magic gets to play the hero, right?"

"Yeah. I'll walk you through it when we get

to the beach, but basically this scene continues from the one we shot this morning. You fall to the ground, and you lie there unconscious. The tide comes in. Magic tries to revive you, but he can't make you open your eyes. When the waves lift you and carry you out to sea, he swims to the rescue."

"That is so cool!" said Kami.

"It's complicated to make Magic understand what we want him to do; I warned Brad that it won't be easy, especially with the time pressure we're under due to the tides. My idea is to swim alongside Magic in rehearsal to show him. Then when we actually shoot the scene, I'll be able to stand on the sideline and yell instructions."

"Magic's very smart," Kami reminded Jack as he chose the same parking space as before and they jumped down from the cab. "He'll pick it up."

"You're okay with the floating out to sea part?" Jack asked. "There'll be boats and lifeguards, plus the guy from the American Humane Association ready and waiting."

"I'm a strong swimmer. I've been swimming in Clearwater Lake since I was four years old, so I'll be fine." She lowered the ramp and stepped inside the trailer. "Come on, Magic, let's get to work."

∾ ◦ ᕐ

*It's weird playing dead at the edge of the ocean and letting waves lap around you,* Kami thought. She had to keep her eyes closed and allow her body to totally relax, trusting the lifeguards in a nearby boat to keep a look out and not let her encounter any real harm.

"So, everyone knows what we're doing, and we're ready for action!" Brad had announced over the sound of waves crashing onto the shore. He'd checked that Jack was in place off camera with Magic, waiting for his cue. Then he'd asked Kami to take up position. Now here she was, lying at the water's edge as if she'd just fallen from her horse, feeling the cold, shallow water lift her as wave after wave met the shore. Then she sensed herself being gently carried out to sea.

It happened fast. The water was surprisingly powerful, raising her up as Jack released Magic and let him splash toward her, calling instructions as he went. She heard the horse wade chest-deep through the breaking waves, felt him nudge her "lifeless" body with his nose. She tried not to react as another strong wave came in and the current carried her away.

*Eyes closed!* she reminded herself. *Trust Jack and Magic to get it right!* There would be a count of ten, then he would be with her again, nudging and pushing, willing her to open her eyes.

Eight, nine, ten. Right on cue she felt Magic swim alongside her. She could finally open her eyes and react. She raised an arm and draped it around his neck, then slowly climbed onto his back. *Slump forward, don't look up. Let Magic swim for the shore.*

The white waves crashed, and the sun beat down from a clear blue sky. Magic swam until his feet hit the bottom and he waded out of the water.

"Good boy," she whispered.

"Cut!" the director called.

Without one misstep, the job was done in a single, successful take.

Kami saw Brad give Jack a high five, and she caught sight of Tom behind them, wearing his baseball cap. *Cool,* she thought. *I'm glad he came.* She smiled at him as he ran forward to take Magic from her while Wanda wrapped her in a beach robe and hurried her off the set.

∽ ◦ ∾

"No way do I believe this is your first stunt-riding job," Nathan said as he sat down at the table to eat supper with Kami, Jack, and Tom. "You were so amazing."

"Kami only came to Stardust Stables at the start of the summer," Jack explained. "She's a fast learner, plus she bonded with her horse right away."

"Stop! I'm embarrassed," Kami pleaded. They'd been talking about her nonstop since they sat down to eat. "Let's change the topic."

"Tom, you're not saying much. Do you want to run through tomorrow's action sequence?" Jack suggested.

Tom shook his head. "I read the script. I already know what we have to do." Pushing his plate away, he stood up and muttered that he had stuff to do.

"Do we know what's wrong with him?" Jack asked Kami as Tom walked out of the dining room. "He's not sick, is he?"

"I don't think so," Kami said. She was about to follow him and find out what the problem was, but Nathan put his hand on her arm.

"What about you? Do you have stuff to do?" he asked quietly.

Surprised by his touch, she felt herself blush, then shook her head.

"Is it okay if I spend some time with Kami tonight, sir?" Nathan asked Jack politely.

Jack nodded. "But it's nine already, and we have an early start tomorrow, so make sure not to stay up too late," he warned. Then he followed after Tom.

Nathan grinned at Kami. "Let's walk," he suggested, leading the way outside.

She followed, heart racing, into the warm, moonlit yard. The sweet scent of jasmine that grew on either side of the ranch-house door filled the air, and they strolled together down the driveway toward the dark forest beyond the gates.

"You're not scared of the dark?" Nathan asked, putting an arm around her shoulder. "Course not, what am I thinking? You're the girl who played dead and risked being carried out to sea."

"No, I'm not scared," she said, trying to match Nathan's long stride. This was unbelievable. She was walking with Nathan Atwood in the moonlight, and he had his arm around her shoulder! *Breathe! Focus!* she told herself. "But I'll tell you what does scare me. Actually, not 'what' but 'who.'"

"Let me guess. We're talking Coreen?" he asked.

"Yeah," Kami said.

"Sorry . . . she went a little crazy earlier."

"I guess it happens a lot?" Kami asked.

By now they were deep in the forest, catching only glimpses of the silver moon through thick pine branches. Kami was surprised to see that her question had thrown Nathan off-balance and made him take his arm away from her shoulder.

"Sorry. Go ahead and tell me it's not my business," she said.

"Don't be sorry. It's just that Coreen may look like a prima donna, and I make jokes about her living up to her star reputation, but actually she isn't usually mean to people the way she was to you earlier today. She must really be on edge about all this horse stuff. Seeing her reaction to Magic made me realize what she must be going through and how we're running out of time."

"Do you two know each other well?" Kami asked.

"We went to acting school together, and we've already been in two movies together as leads, playing brother and sister. *Moonlight Dream* is our third — the first where we have a romantic connection."

"You're really close," Kami decided, increasingly intrigued by the fact that Coreen Kessler, the girl who seemed to have it all, had problems like anyone else.

"Since Coreen first freaked out over riding the horse at your stables, she's blown the whole thing out of proportion. She's turned it into some kind of phobia. When Brad finds out, she'll be in serious trouble," Nathan confided. "But, Kami, I still think you could help her."

"Only if she'll let me," she said. She sighed,

recalling Jack's advice. They fell silent in the thick darkness of the forest, and then she spoke again. "Do you know where Coreen is now?"

"I saw her before dinner. She said she wasn't hungry and went straight to her room," Nathan replied.

There was another long silence while Kami turned back and retraced her steps with Nathan at her side. "Go get her," she told him as they reached the iron gates at the entrance to Five Sisters. "Don't say anything, just bring her out to the meadow. No questions, just go!"

∿ ◦ ℮

"You know, people have problems," Kami told Magic when she found him munching at the feeder in the meadow. "We humans make life more complicated than you equines."

Magic snorted, then went on munching hay.

"It's what we do. Take me and Nathan, for example. My heart went crazy for those ten seconds when he put his arm around my shoulder. Me and Nathan Atwood! But I get it — he likes me, but only as a friend. I can tell by the way he talks about Coreen, kind of intense and serious, that he really, really cares about her!"

Magic munched some more.

"See, life's really easy for you. But take Coreen as another example. You saw how she was with you out here earlier — that girl has a total fear of horses."

Hearing something in the distance, Magic looked up and pricked his ears, his dark eyes glistening in the moonlight.

"What is it?" Kami strained her ears to hear. "Oh, it's Legend calling." She glanced around. The palomino was missing from the meadow, so Tom must have taken her for a ride under the stars. She turned back to Magic, stroking his ears. "Forget Legend, and listen to me. Coreen has a problem, and she's too proud to ask for help. But tomorrow's crunch time, and she can't hide it any longer."

Magic tilted his head to one side in his usual way.

"Listen, I have a plan . . ."

∽ ◦ ◡

Kami was still waiting for Coreen and Nathan when Tom and Legend returned. They stopped at the gates to the meadow. The palomino's pale mane and tail seemed to sparkle like silver in the moonlight as it swished back and forth with contentment.

"Hey, where have you been?" Kami called.

"I wanted some alone time, so we went down to the beach to watch the waves," Tom said.

"Mesmerizing, huh?" Kami walked to the gate and opened it for them.

Tom nodded. "I could watch them forever."

This was the first time Kami had talked with Tom in what felt like ages, and she was glad to break down some of those awkward silences. "Magic heard Legend calling," she said.

He nodded. "We cantered through the shallow waves. Legend loved it."

Kami smiled. "I wish I'd been there with Magic."

"Maybe next time," Tom said as he rode Legend toward the feeder at the far side of the meadow.

∽ ◦ ℃

"Walk and talk," Nathan told Coreen, as he steered her toward the meadow at the far side of the ranch house. "Come on, Cori, share with me."

"What's there to talk about?" she asked miserably.

"You, your amazing career — everything," Nathan said.

"My so-called career is about to make a U-turn, and you know it."

"Not necessarily," he argued.

"Yes, necessarily. You read our contracts — working with horses is part of the deal. I should have told my agent 'no way' from the start."

"Okay, but you didn't, and so here we are," Nathan said. He stopped beside the makeup trailer and took both of Coreen's hands in his. "What do you want to do? Do you want me to go find Brad, tell him you're wimping out?"

"I am not wimping out!" Suddenly fiery, Coreen pulled her hands free.

"That's what everyone will say — 'Coreen Kessler had a meltdown. Kessler can't take the pressure. Coreen's career on the rocks.'"

She slowly let out a long, deep breath and then quickly inhaled, pulling back her shoulders. "Okay, Mr. Know-It-All, I'm not — I repeat, I am *not* — wimping out!"

"So?" he asked, grinning.

"So, I am rising to the challenge," she insisted, head up, shoulders back, taking more deep breaths.

"How?"

"By confronting my demons and beating my phobia," Coreen responded.

"Like an arachnophobe learning to love spiders?" Nathan asked.

"Exactly like that," Coreen insisted. "Find Kami. Get her to introduce me to the gray horse!"

And she strode ahead of Nathan toward the meadow.

∽ ◦ ⌣

"Come with me, here in the middle," Kami invited Coreen to stand beside her. "Take this rope. I'll need you to snake the loose end through the dirt, like this."

Nervously, Coreen took the rope and released one end experimentally along the ground.

"Good. Okay, gather it up again. Now we walk up to Magic. We don't make eye contact — horses read that as an aggressive act." Kami crossed the meadow with Coreen until they stood roughly the rope's length away from Magic.

"This is way too close." Coreen shook from head to toe. "He's so big, and I have no clue what he's about to do."

"Look at Magic's ears," Kami told her. "They're perked up and pointed forward. That means he's alert, wondering what you're going to ask him to do. If his ears are flat against his head and his nostrils flare out, he's scared and getting ready to run. We don't want him to be scared. We want him to listen. It looks like he's ready now. Release the rope again and snake it toward his back feet."

Coreen followed Kami's instruction, and the

sudden movement along the ground pushed Magic forward into a canter.

"Keep behind him, keep him moving," Kami urged.

Coreen snaked the rope again, surprised that the horse understood the long-distance command.

"Use the rope, keep him going until he starts to lower his head."

"I don't touch him with the rope?" Coreen asked.

"No, and don't look at his eyes. Keep him cantering."

Coreen nodded and kept on working with Magic, Kami walking alongside.

After ten minutes, Kami spoke again. "Okay, now Magic's head is going down — he's tired. Ease off with the rope, let him slow to a walk. Good. Now half turn away from him. Look, he's walking on, sticking close to the fence, but he's turning toward you and wondering what you want him to do next. You're going to ease up completely and let him get near you."

"Get near me?" Coreen echoed, sounding like this was still her worst nightmare.

"It's okay, you've worked him hard. He recognizes you're the boss, like the alpha male in a big herd. Now all he wants is to come close and be your friend," Kami explained.

"My friend?" Coreen repeated, still unsure.

"Yeah, you're in control, remember. No eye contact, just turn away a little more," Kami instructed. "Look, now he feels safe to approach you. His head's down. You're still the boss."

"Don't be scared, Cori." Nathan stood by the gate, his eyes glued on Coreen. "You can do it." He spoke under his breath so as not to break her concentration.

"Magic is stepping into your space. He's saying 'please let me in,'" Kami said, smiling at Coreen. She'd used this technique a hundred times with new colts back home at Elk Creek. "So raise your hand slowly, eyes down, still don't look at him. Stroke him, say hi."

Slowly, Coreen raised her hand to stroke Magic's neck. "So soft, so warm," she murmured, her voice full of wonder. "And so gentle."

"That's horses for you," Kami said softly. She grinned and stroked Magic's neck. They'd done it; Coreen had taken a first step on the road to conquering her horse phobia once and for all.

*Thank you, Magic. Thank you for being you,* Kami thought.

# Chapter 10

"So, guys, we have a tight schedule," Brad announced early the next morning as he gathered the crew on the beach.

Jack, Kami, and Tom had unloaded Legend and Magic from the trailer in time to hear the director's team talk.

"First, we shoot scene forty-three with Coreen and Nathan, plus the two horses," Brad explained. Glancing around, he noted the absence of Coreen as usual. "Where is she? Will someone tell her to get her butt down here now?"

As an assistant drove back to Five Sisters to hurry her along, Brad continued to give instructions. "Forty-three is where Moonlight carries Krystal back to the house — she's half drowned, remember. So, Nathan, you ride the palomino through the dunes and see that she's in trouble. You catch up with her and warn her that you heard her dad tell the horse dealer to come back later. The scene ends with Matt stepping off the porch, looking mean as hell."

"Now all we need is Coreen," Jack muttered. The horses were ready, and everyone was in place except for her. "Tom, you can hand Legend over to Nathan for this scene. Check her cinch first. Kami, be ready to hand Magic over to Coreen."

Kami waited anxiously. Coreen's no-show surprised her, and now she wasn't so sure how much last night's lesson had helped after all. One glance at Nathan's worried face told her he feared the same thing. But then she relaxed — a silver SUV had arrived at the parking lot, and Coreen stepped out, looking tense.

After that, everything happened fast. Brad checked camera angles one final time, Tom gave Nathan a leg up into the saddle, Wanda sprayed water over Coreen's blue dress to replicate the near-drowning episode, and finally Coreen approached Kami and Magic.

"Coreen, we're all set up," Brad told her. "The light's perfect. Come on, let's shoot!"

"Ready?" Kami prompted, offering to help her into the saddle.

For a moment, Coreen hesitated. There was a big difference between bonding with Magic in a quiet, moonlit meadow and actually climbing up onto the horse in the bright light of day in front of all these people. She turned to Nathan for support and saw him nod calmly and urge her on. "I'm ready," she decided.

*Good work!* Kami thought as she helped Coreen onto Magic's back. "Lean forward," she instructed. "Put both arms around Magic's neck and let him carry you slowly toward the house. Remember — trust him!"

"I can't believe I'm doing this!" Coreen groaned as she felt Magic's weight shift beneath her. But she did what Kami told her as they waited for the cameras to roll.

"Go, girl!" Kami whispered as she stepped away. "Magic will look out for you. Nothing bad will happen."

*Scene forty-three, take one. Action!*

Magic carried Coreen up the beach. The camera caught her beautiful face in close-up, eyes closed, head resting against the horse's dark mane. It stayed on her as Nathan caught up with her before she reached the house. Coreen heard him call her name, and she opened her eyes, raising her head from Magic's neck.

*Cut! Take two.*

Rearrange Coreen's wet hair so that stray strands streak across her cheek. Tone down the mascara, enhance the paleness of her cheeks. Spray more water on the dress. Action!

*Cut! Take three, take four . . .*

Brad wanted the scene to be perfect. He altered camera angles to include more of Magic's face. He asked Coreen to slump more to one side as though she were in danger of falling off.

*Take five . . .*

"I'm amazed," Jack admitted to Kami and Tom as they watched off camera. "No way does that girl look like she has a problem with horses."

"She doesn't — not anymore," Kami answered with a satisfied smile. *Crisis totally over,* she thought. *Coreen's glittering career is back on course.*

"Good, I got what I need," Brad decided at last. "Coreen, Nathan, take a break while we set up for the reverse shots. And thanks, guys. You both did a great job."

∽ ◦ ୬

Brad worked the Stardust team hard during their remaining days on set at Five Sisters.

On Wednesday afternoon, he jumped ahead to scene seventy-eight and shot a sequence where Kami and Tom cantered through the forest. This was the part in the *Moonlight Dream* plot after Coreen and Nathan's characters had decided to snatch Moonlight from his stable before the trailer could return to take him away to the sale barn.

Kami, doubling for Coreen, had to ride Magic bareback and with just a rope halter. The head wrangler, Scott, made sure that Kami was okay with this, then gave her the go-ahead and watched her swerve between trees and duck under low branches on their flight from Mean Dad and the horse dealer.

Thursday morning was scene eighty-one — another forest scene where the runaways rode deeper into the forest and came across a logging operation at work. Tom and Kami had to ride Legend and Magic past sawing machinery and through an area where giant trees had been felled, climbing their way over trunks until a tree crashed down close to where they rode, spooking the horses.

"Legend and Magic are in a blind panic," Jack reminded them before the call for action. "They're out of control, jumping those high log piles to your left. The camera follows you as you jump. Tom, you get to the third pile, then Legend hits the logs, and you fall. Kami, you get Magic over the logs but you turn and go back for Tom."

It was a tricky stunt, especially since Kami rode without saddle or bridle, and the territory was risky. No horse liked jumping over high, solid logs and cantering through undergrowth. She hoped they could do it in one take.

"Let's get through this safely," she murmured to Magic as they waited for the director's call. "Then we can go back to the ranch and chill."

Magic nickered as if to say, *"Stick with me."*

Next to her, Tom waited nervously with Legend.

She smiled at him, glad when he smiled back. "Cool hat," she said, grinning, thinking how good he looked in the beaten-up, dusty Stetson from Wanda's shelves. Then she settled her own straw hat more firmly on her head and turned up the collar of her checked shirt the way Wanda had told her to.

"Likewise," he muttered.

Tom still wasn't talking much, even after their late-night conversation in the meadow, and this made her sad. Then again, maybe he was always like this on set, just serious and focused.

*What happened to the old jokey Tom?* She'd wanted to ask that pretty much ever since they had arrived at Five Sisters. But Tom's walls were up, and it looked as if she'd have to wait until they got back to Stardust before she found out the answer. *I'll ask Kellie,* she thought. *His sister will know how to get him to lighten up.*

The thought had hardly registered before Brad gave the two young stunt riders the go-ahead. Tom and Kami set off side by side, ambling between trees at a relaxed trot until the signal came for them to make their horses rear and run. There was no actual logging machinery on set and no scary chainsaws, so the two riders had to fake a reaction and set their horses into spook mode.

"Let's go, Magic!" Kami hissed as he rose onto his hind legs, plunged down, then set off on a wild canter through the thick undergrowth. Their every move was captured from above by a camera mounted on a crane.

Tom and Legend kept pace, both horses clearing the first and second log piles with ease.

"So far, so good!" Kami murmured. Magic's trot was smooth and safe. He soared high over the logs and landed evenly, forging on toward the next.

But the third pile was where Tom and Legend faked the fall. Kami felt them next to her, caught their blurred shape out of the corner of her eye, saw the obstacle loom up ahead.

*Wham!* Horse and rider were down, rolling on the ground in a controlled fall. She wheeled Magic around in time to see Legend go belly up with her legs in the air and Tom lying motionless.

"Cut!" Brad called.

Kami and Magic trotted back to the scene of the "accident." "Okay, Tom, you heard what he said," Kami called. "You can get up now."

Legend rolled, folded her legs under her and stood up. Tom lay still.

"Tom!" Kami quickly slid to the ground and bent over him. "Tom, get up!"

For a moment everything stopped.

Then Tom opened one eye. "Gotcha!" he shouted, grinning as he jumped to his feet.

∽ ◦ ᘐ

"That was so not funny!" Kami was still not over the scare Tom had given her earlier. Even now, as they walked Magic and Legend out to the meadow at the end of the day, she was on edge. "All week you've been acting like the sulky kid at the back of the class, and now suddenly you're the joker again."

Tom laughed as they took off the horses' halters and watched them make a run for the fresh alfalfa. "You should've seen the look on your face!" he said.

"Seriously, I thought my heart was going to jump out of my chest," Kami complained, closing the gate after them. "I don't know what's gotten into you lately — moody one minute, playing tricks on me the next."

"Nothing's gotten into me," he said with a shrug.

"Yes, it has. You're different," Kami said.

"No, I'm not."

"You didn't even come to see my very first scene on the beach," she reminded him.

Tom gave another shrug. "I didn't think you'd noticed."

"What? Why not?" said Kami.

Tom shrugged and looked a little embarrassed.

"Well, I did. I also noticed that you've basically stopped speaking to me since then," Kami said.

"I told you, I've had things to do," Tom replied.

"And now you play dead and scare me half to death! What was *that* all about?"

"I don't know. I guess I couldn't resist."

Kami sighed. *Jeez, this is like pulling teeth,* she thought. She was almost glad to hear footsteps and see Coreen hurrying to join them.

Tom saw her too. "Catch you later," he told Kami and quickly slipped away.

"I hope you're giving your horse plenty to eat," Coreen said cheerfully. She took her phone out of her pocket and snapped a photo of Magic tucking into his evening meal. "So cute!" she said, beaming. "I'm going to put the pictures on Facebook . . . show the whole world how beautiful he is."

Kami smiled back. "How many friends do you have on Facebook?"

"Over a million."

"You hear that, Magic — a million! You're going to be famous!"

"And I'll tell everyone you're a terrific rider," Coreen promised. "I'll even come clean and tell them I was terrified of horses until you came along and cured me."

"You don't have to do that," Kami told her. "I'm just happy it worked out."

Putting away her phone, Coreen's face grew serious. "No, really, I want to say sorry for being a total nightmare. Can you forget the nasty stuff I said to you?"

"You were under pressure," Kami said.

"Yeah. I didn't mean what I said," Coreen explained.

"That's okay. I understand."

"And I want to say thank you, Kami."

"Thank Nathan, too. It was his idea," Kami reminded her.

Coreen nodded. "Nathan knows me better than anyone. We grew up together."

"He told me. You know he really cares about you, right?" Kami asked.

"I do." Coreen's smile was wistful at first, then her mouth twitched and turned mischievous. "So, Kami, how about you and Tom?"

"Tom?" Kami blushed, surprised that it had

been so obvious. "Not the same," she insisted. "We didn't meet until I joined the stunt-riding team. Tom doesn't know me well at all."

"No?" Coreen refused to step aside as Kami tried to get past.

"No. You've seen him lately," Kami said. "He hardly even speaks to me."

"But he looks at you plenty. When you're practicing stunts with Jack, Tom watches you like a hawk. And when he sees you talking with Nathan, he turns around and walks the other way."

"He does?" Kami blushed even more.

"He walks away because he's jealous," Coreen insisted.

"No, he can't be!" Flustered, Kami refused to believe it.

Coreen's smile broadened. "Let me spell it out slowly," she said. "In words of one syllable so that you get it. Kami, Tom — likes — you. Period."

$\sim\!\!\!\!\sim\; \circ\; \backsim$

Kami was shell-shocked. Could what first Kellie and now Coreen told her actually be true? And was that why jokey Tom had turned into Moody Boy all of a sudden? She had to find out, but it took all her courage to go looking for him later that evening.

"Ask me to do a saddle fall, Roman riding, a back vault, a drag, a front wing — I don't care how many bruises I get. I would rather do anything other than this," she muttered to Magic as she looked out at the meadow. "What if it turns out that Kellie and Coreen got it wrong? What if he laughs? How stupid will I feel!"

Magic listened, then tilted his head.

"But I have to talk to him," she decided, turning away from the gate and spotting Tom in the entrance to the barn. She swallowed hard and walked over.

Tom didn't react as she approached — just leaned against the doorpost, hat pulled down over his forehead and arms folded.

"So," she began. "Tomorrow we pack up and fly home. We let Scott Maxwell's other stand-in horses take over from here."

Tom raised an eyebrow.

"I can't wait to see Kellie and the girls again. Even Becca. I texted her, and she says Pepper's leg is healing okay." *Whoa, this is hard work.* Kami still wasn't getting a reaction, so she blabbed more nonsense about calling home to find out how Buttercup was doing without her and if Squeaky had had her kittens yet. "Sorry, I'm an idiot," she ended breathlessly. "I don't usually ramble on and on . . ."

"Yeah, don't waste your breath on me," Tom mumbled, turning away and checking out Legend's tack hanging on a nearby hook. "Go find Nathan and say your goodbyes, exchange phone numbers, leave him your email address, whatever."

"Nathan?" It was true. Tom was jealous! "You don't think he . . . I don't . . . We aren't . . ."

"Come on, Kami, spit it out," he said.

"Nathan and I do not like each other," she said. "That's stupid."

"Well, thanks for calling me stupid," he grunted.

"No, that's not what I meant at all." Talk about digging a deeper hole — this one was big enough to bury herself in. She took a long breath and tried to explain more calmly. "Sure, I had a crush on him, just like you did with Coreen. Who could help it?"

"I watched you. It looked like more than a schoolgirl crush," Tom muttered.

"Yeah, well, if you'd been around more, you'd know that Nathan doesn't act like a big movie star. In fact, he's an all-around nice guy. He knew this was my first stunt-riding job, so he showed me the ropes, helped me settle in. That's all."

Tom cleared his throat. "It's cool, Kami," he said. "I was out of line with the Nathan comment. Forget I said anything."

"What I'm saying is — oh gosh, I don't know what I'm saying!" Kami said. She was done; she didn't know how to make things better. She backed out of the barn, shaking her head.

"Kami." Tom let her get halfway across the yard before he spoke.

She turned.

He came right up to her and slowly leaned in, locking eyes with her. "You want to ride along the beach with me?" he asked.

∽ ◦ ∾

Legend and Magic matched each other stride for stride. They trotted along the water's edge as the sun sank over the flat, sparkling horizon.

Kami sat deep in the saddle, hair blowing free, hearing the splash of the horses' hooves and the call of gulls overhead. She glanced at Tom, whose Stetson was still low on his forehead, and he smiled back at her.

"Race you to the rocks," he suggested.

"You hear that, Magic?" Kami whispered, loosening her reins and letting him run free.

Her horse exploded out of a canter and into a gallop, surging forward and kicking up spray. Beside them, neck and neck, Tom crouched low in the saddle like a racehorse jockey. The dappled gray versus the palomino, silhouetted against the red setting sun, only slowing to a stop as they ran out of white sand and came to the rocky, forested headland.

"Dead heat?" Kami asked, leaning forward to pat Magic's neck.

Tom grinned and nodded. "A photo finish for sure."

Together they turned their horses and started the long walk back along the sand.

# Chapter 11

"Kami and Magic did an okay job," Jack reported to Lizzie.

It was late Friday afternoon, and everyone was hanging out at Stardust Stables, listening to Jack's feedback. The horses were fed and watered, taking a well-earned rest after their long trip home.

"Only 'okay'?" Kami whispered to Alisa. "Not even 'good'?"

"Don't stress — he's playing down the praise because he doesn't want your head to grow too big for your hat," Alisa whispered. "We can't afford a new one!"

Kellie agreed. "'Okay' from Jack is the most anyone ever gets around here."

Lizzie smiled at Kami, then came over and gave her a quick hug. "I knew you could do it," she said.

Kami grinned back. Boy, was she glad she and Magic were home and in one piece.

"A star in the making!" Hayley said, smiling.

"So, how was Nathan Atwood in the flesh?" Kellie chipped in.

The girls had run to meet Kami as she got off the trailer, desperate for an update. They had all helped take care of the two horses and then crowded around her, begging for details on the *Moonlight Dream* shoot. They'd mostly ignored Tom, who was, of course, an old hand at stunt riding.

"Yeah, Kami, is Nathan as much of a hunk as he is in his movies?" Alisa asked.

"Totally. Anyway, you saw him here in the corral — swoon factor ten out of ten," said Kami.

"No hidden flaws?" Alisa pressed.

"Not one. The opposite, actually," Kami replied.

"Oh, poor Tom," Kellie said. She sighed, turning to him. "Nathan perfect this, Nathan screen-god that. How can a humble stunt rider compete?"

"Not possible," Tom agreed, avoiding looking at Kami.

"Quit teasing your brother," Hayley told Kellie.

"Actually, it's no contest," Kami told the girls. Smiling, she stole a quick glance at Tom.

∽ ◦ ℃

"So Pepper's leg is healing," Becca told Kami.

It was later that evening, and they were standing by the row of stalls where Kami had first set eyes on Magic. Pepper stuck his head over the stable wall, looking for sympathy, which the two girls gave him in spades.

"The vet says no more painkillers but still to rest it for a week. After that, we're back in action, aren't we, Pepper?" Becca asked.

Kami rubbed Pepper's nose. "Great news. And what about Pete Mason?"

"Shh! Don't even say that name around here."

"Didn't the cops do anything?" Kami asked.

"The sheriff went to his place to 'talk' with him. Mason swore he was nowhere near Stardust Stables when our horses broke loose, and he has an alibi, so it's Tom's and your word against his," Becca explained. "Which means he's still out there, free to carry on with his campaign to sabotage Stardust."

"Not good," Kami said, sighing.

"The sheriff did warn him, though," Becca went on. "He said they would be keeping a close eye on him for the next few weeks."

"Better."

"Lizzie was in shock at first — even she didn't think her ex would play that dirty. But now she just shrugs and says 'don't look back,'" Becca reported. "She's a glass-half-full person. Anyway, we did get new business contracts while you were away."

"Hey, you two!" Hayley walked by with a bucket of grain for Cool Kid, who was stabled two stalls farther down the row, greedily looking out for his extra feed. "Kellie said for you to join her, Ross, and Alisa by the soda machine. They want to celebrate."

So Kami and Becca gave Pepper a final pat, then crossed the yard in the last of the day's sunshine.

"So what new contracts do we have?" Kami asked Kellie as she and Becca joined the small group sitting around the table under the yellow umbrella.

"Dylan and I got the cattle-rustling TV series, remember?" Kellie said, her broad smile almost splitting her face in two. "We trailer Dylan out to Texas later this summer."

"And Diabolo and I auditioned and got a 'maybe' for the *Wildfire* movie," Alisa reported. "We should hear for sure after the weekend."

Kami nodded happily, then silently wondered where her next job would take her and Magic — California again, New Mexico, Canada . . .

Whatever it was, wherever they went, they sure would work hard to improve their vault tricks and shoulder stands, their front wings and one-foot drags. "It's going to be a great summer," she said.

*With a great team,* she added to herself as the group split off to do laundry, sweep the tack room, and scoop poop before supper.

She waved at Tom and Zak riding the tractor, taking alfalfa out to the meadow, and then she crossed the yard and climbed over the gate to follow after them. Magic spotted her and trotted over to meet her.

"Happy to be home?" Kami asked, sitting astride the gate and reaching out to stroke him.

He ducked his head and snorted.

"Me too," Kami said. She sighed, not wanting to change a thing as she watched the sun slip down behind the mountains and listened as the valley gradually fell silent. "I'm totally happy with my life, right here, right now."

## About the Author

Sable Hamilton is the pen name for Jenny Oldfield, author of a wide range of books for children and young adults — including the internationally successful mini series Beautiful Dead and Dark Angel. With Stardust Stables, she has returned to one of her favorite subjects — the glamour, the thrills, and the trials of working with horses!

# Glossary

**arrogant** (AR-uh-guhnt) — when a person acts like or thinks they are better than everyone else

**concentrate** (KAHN-suhn-trate) — to focus your thoughts and attention on one thing

**demonstrate** (DEM-uhn-strate) — to show how to do something, to show something clearly

**lame** (LAYM) — having trouble walking because of sickness or an injury

**mischievous** (MIS-chuh-vuhs) — playfully annoying or teasing

**sabotage** (SAB-uh-tahzh) — damaging property or doing something bad on purpose in order to stop something from happening

**scout** (SKOUT) — a person that looks for new talent or for someone that could work well in a certain job

**stamina** (STAM-uh-nuh) — the energy to be able to do something over a long period of time

**swoon** (SWOON) — to faint or become weak or dizzy because of great emotion

**undercut** (UHN-der-kuht) — to offer a lower price than someone else who is selling the same thing

# More about Horses

**bridle** (BRYE-duhl) — a harness that goes on a horse's head, which allows a person to control and guide it

**canter** (KAN-tur) — a medium-fast speed, faster than a trot but slower than a gallop

**currycomb** (KUR-ee-kohm) — a type of comb with plastic ridges used to get dirt and other things out of a horse's coat

**halter** (HAWL-tur) — a strap that fits behind the ears and over the nose, used to lead or tie up an animal like a horse

**lope** (LOHP) — a Western term for canter, but may be more easy-going and relaxed than a canter

**palomino** (pal-uh-MEE-noh) — a horse with a golden coat and white mane and tail

**sorrel** (SOR-uhl) — a horse that is reddish brown with a mane and tail of the same or lighter color

**tack** (TAK) — all of the things you need to ride a horse, like a saddle and bridle

**trot** (TRAHT) — a speed that's in between walking and running, slower than a canter or gallop

# Discussion Questions

1. Kami felt homesick during her first week at Stardust Stables. Have you ever felt homesick? What did you do to feel better? Talk about it.

2. Coreen used to be scared of horses, but she learned to like them. Is there something that you were once afraid of, but aren't anymore? How did you get over your fear?

3. Why do you think Tom was so moody on set? Discuss possible reasons, using examples from the story.

# Writing Prompts

1. Kami was nervous when she first arrived at Stardust Stables. Think of a time when you were the new kid or were nervous about starting something. Write about your experience.

2. Write about how Becca and Kami's relationship changed throughout the story. What was it like at the beginning? What was it like at the end? What caused the change?

3. The stunt riders at Stardust Stables get to meet a lot of celebrities. If you could hang out with any celebrity for one day, who would it be? Write a story about what you and that person would do.

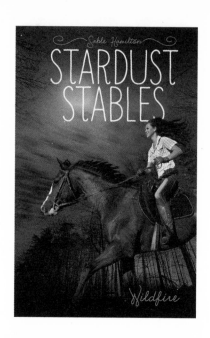

# Wildfire

Seasoned stunt rider Alisa can't wait to start work on *Wildfire* where she'll be doubling for Hollywood A-lister Hannah Hart. She and Diabolo, her beautiful mare, have been specially chosen for the job because of Diabolo's fearlessness around fire. Alisa is riding high until she spots her old adversary, Lucy Reeves, on set. Lucy is stunt riding for a rival stable and it looks like she's out to cause trouble . . .

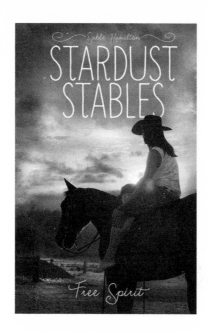

# Free Spirit

Kellie and her horse, Dylan, are up in the mountains of Colorado filming a low-budget movie about pioneers in the 1800s. The location is so remote that the cast and crew are camping out in tents, and Kellie's enjoying being part of the team. But when disaster suddenly strikes, there's only one person who can save the day. Does Kellie have what it takes to step into the spotlight?